UNDER MY MASTER'S WINGS

'Give me your hand.' I turned up my right palm behind my back and David squirted lube onto my fingers. 'Put your finger in your ass.' Slowly I obeyed orders as David thrust to his own rhythm. 'Put my dick inside,' he finally whispered in my ear, tugging my finger from the hole. I reached around for his slick erection and David helped me help him inside. 'Push down,' he groaned.

It was like a wild animal had been released. A jackhammer actually would have been more bearable. The only thing that stopped me from crying mercy were the sweet and tender kisses David was showering all over my back and neck. Unfortunately, my tight asshole didn't care what the hell was going on with any of my other body parts. 'Mercy!' I shouted when finally I could take no more. David flipped me over, single-handedly securing my legs above my head. Then he forced his fat cock back inside – my ass. 'Ow! It hurts!' I whimpered through clenched teeth.

David held still to meet my eyes with a look that lied *this is hurting me more than it is you*.

'You need to be punished,' he quietly explained.

UNDER MY MASTER'S WINGS

Lauren Wissot

The LAST
WORD *in*
FETISH

nexus

enthusiast

This book is a work of fiction.
In real life, make sure you practise safe, sane and
consensual sex.

First published in 2006 by
Nexus Enthusiast
Nexus
Thames Wharf Studios
Rainville Road
London W6 9HA

www.nexus-books.co.uk

A catalogue record for this book is available from the British
Library.

ISBN 0 352 34042 8
ISBN 9 780352 340429

MIX
Paper | Supporting
responsible forestry
FSC® C018179

Typeset by TW Typesetting, Plymouth, Devon

The Random House Group Limited supports The Forest Stewardship
Council (FSC®), the leading international forest certification organisation.
Our books carrying the FSC label are printed on FSC® certified paper.
FSC is the only forest certification scheme endorsed by the leading
environmental organisations, including Greenpeace. Our
paper procurement policy can be found at
www.randomhouse.co.uk/environment

Printed and bound in Great Britain by Clays Ltd, St Ives PLC

February 2000

Last night I had a dream I was in a relationship with Italian porn legend Rocco Siffredi. Must be the result of all the cocksucking and anal sex I've been engaging in lately – the triple X equivalent of spicy food before bed, I guess.

David was back in NYC. I arrived home from work on February 1st to find a heavily French-accented message on my answering machine.

'Hello, Lauren. It's David from Montreal. I'm in town for the week. I'm staying at the Comfort Inn in Room 204 so you can call me if you like. Or I'll call you tonight. It's noon on Tuesday. Bye.'

I raced around my apartment screaming like a banshee. My next-door neighbour must have thought I'd hit the lottery – and, in the world of gay male fantasy, I suppose I had.

It all began just two months ago.

Contents

The Training

(December 1999)

My friend Jimmy and I had made Wednesday plans to go to the Gaiety Theater on 46th Street – the only place left to see live male strippers in Giuliani's Disneyfied Deuce. If I wasn't going dancing, watching naked men do it for me seemed the next best thing.

Of course I had an ulterior motive. My sister had gone the week before with her gay pal Matt and she had been the toast of the club – getting approached by not one but *three* hot male strippers. Much to my delight, she informed me that most of the strippers were straight, strictly 'gay for pay', buff and totally aggressive in their approach. These guys were walking up to her, handing her phone numbers and saying things like, 'Did you see my show? I was the one with the big dick!' and 'Call me. I have to have you!' In other words, they were completely my type. And best of all – they'd fuck girls for free!

At least biologically female ones – and I definitely fit that description. With my long brown hair and petite frame I could pass as a Parker Posey-type party girl into casual sex. These guys wouldn't stick around long enough to discover the truth: that I was really an undercover agent in the mainstream world, a gay boy born into female form. (I'd always hated the term 'Gender Identity Disorder', as if being transgendered, two-spirited, was a sickness, something to be cured with hormone pills and operations. The Native American communities never pushed their two-spirited members to have sex changes, to conform. Why was my being mismatched something that needed to be fixed?)

Indecisive about my gender in the womb, I'd chosen both sexes – which put me in the unusual position of inhabiting a biologically female body, yet having not a clue as to what it felt like to be female. Lately I'd become tired of fighting this disjunction, certainly not willing to take up arms of hormone pills and operations, so I'd come to accept my experience as necessary, a requisite path. I was off to scale a mountain of men through sex, trying on different bodies like items of clothing, in order to claim my own manhood at the peak. I made sure to only fuck guys I wanted to be.

It was 'Immaculate Conception' day according to my calendar. I was wearing my lucky red dress, all high hem and low neckline, that got me laid the last two times I wore it, as I stood on the corner of 46th and Broadway waiting for Jimmy. We paid our twelve bucks each and walked into the small dingy theatre with the tacky silver-tassled stage that looked like it had been decorated by some sad pre-Stonewall queen. We found two seats near the back of the all-male, all-old-fart crowd and awaited dancer number one.

Jimmy and I were quite impressed with the first stripper – a buff, blond all-American boy who probably would have made more tips if he'd come out in a sailor's suit – until we saw the second guy, a muscle-bound Latino with an enormous to-die-for dick. But then we scratched him too off our list when dancer number three appeared. Number three made the first two look like complete amateurs.

This guy was dark, buff, totally hot, and knew that he knew how to work it. He was chomping away on a piece of gum like he was daring the audience to tell him to spit it out, making sexy eye contact one minute and then shooting a smooth smile the next. He was having so much fun stroking his thick nine inches during the second number you wanted to try it, too. Or at least I did. Yup, Jimmy and I agreed we were not leaving the theatre until we met Mr Gum Chewer.

We sat through a couple more cookie cutter Schwarzenegger wannabes with identically sculpted bodies and porn-sized cocks until number six appeared. I grabbed Jimmy's arm as he made his entrance in cop uniform and appropriate corporal attitude. By the time he stripped off his belt and started wielding it as a faux-weapon, Jimmy and I had determined that he too was definitely on our list of strippers to strike up a conversation with.

After the last dancer had flashed his dick and the intermission porno had been projected onto the back screen, Jimmy and I adjourned to the lounge area where you could – uh – mingle with the dancers and set up 'private sessions'. Jimmy and I were waiting like pathetic groupies for the gum chewer and police-man to come from backstage. When neither showed and we were stuck in a room full of young blond all-American boys who no one seemed to want, I told Jimmy I had to go to the bathroom and he had to come with me to block the door. I got up from my seat in the lounge and was making my way over to the men's room when I spotted the gum chewer. Quickly I glanced back through the red velvet curtains that separated the bathroom area from the lounge and caught his eye.

'What have we here?' the gum chewer inquired, parting the curtains like Dracula's cape. He looked me up and down like he was appraising a fine jewel or shopping for a slab of meat.

'Hi.' I smiled at him. 'How are you?'

'Much better now. Where are you going?'

I laughed. 'To the bathroom – although it's pretty disgusting in there.'

'You can use my bathroom.'

'Really? Where's that?'

'Three blocks away.' He pronounced 'three' like 'tree' so I knew that English wasn't his first language. Still, I couldn't place the sexy foreign accent.

'Where? Your hotel room?'

'I have an apartment that my friend loans me when I'm in town. He uses my condo when he's working in Quebec.'

'Really?' I noticed Jimmy listening to our conversation, intently wondering if he too was going to get a piece of the action. Good friend that I am, I decided to help move things along. 'Jimmy, look! It's the gum chewer.' Then I turned back to the gorgeous stripper. 'Are you inviting *us* back to your apartment to use your bathroom?'

'Uh, no. I was just kidding,' he replied nervously as he eyed Jimmy. Then he quickly excused himself, saying he had to get ready for his second show.

'Oh, shit. I fucked up!' I told Jimmy as we found ourselves *sans* stripper. 'Looks like we'll have to go back and wait for the policeman.'

I used the bathroom and then Jimmy and I returned to the lounge. Dancers strutted back and forth but there was no sign of the cop. Suddenly, though, I turned to see that our gum chewer had returned. Ah – a second chance! Immediately I smiled at him and he joined us.

'You're back and all ready to perform?'

'Yup. I've got my gum so I'm all set,' he replied, chomping away.

'I'm Lauren.' I pulled my coat off the empty seat next to me as he took my hand.

'David.'

'This is Jimmy.'

They shook hands and David sat down. As we chatted I learned he was from Quebec City, did construction work in Canada in the summer and spent the rest of the year working the gay male dance circuit around North America. I also found out he was a Pisces and exactly eleven months younger than I was.

'I'm an Aries. Pisces, huh? That's bad,' I sighed. 'No, I'm just kidding. I don't know shit about astrology actually.'

'I do,' David stated. 'Aries – tough people to get along with but good for sex.'

'True,' I agreed, flattering myself.

'Well, I have to go backstage and get ready now. Are you staying?'

'Yeah, for a little while. Listen – I'd really like to take you out for coffee or something while you're in town if you'd be interested.'

'Sure, I'll give you my number.' David took out a pen and small notepad, scratched down his name and number then ripped out the page. 'Why don't you call me tonight? Around twelve-thirty?'

5

'Uh, sure,' I said surprised at how easy this all was.

David left and Jimmy congratulated me on a job well done. Then I went to the pay phone across from the video game to call Roxanne. If I was going to be stuck in Times Square until twelve-thirty I figured I might as well swing by her place for a while. Jimmy had to get up early for work anyway so we made our exit, Jimmy heading for the subway and I for Roxanne's.

I arrived at Roxanne's pink-coloured pad shortly after midnight and recounted the evening's events for her until the clock ticked half past twelve and I had to make my call.

'Hello?' a male voice answered.

'Is David there?'

'Yeah. It's me.'

'Hey, it's Lauren. What are you doing?' I asked, butterflies flapping away in my stomach.

'Rolling a joint and waiting for your call.'

'He's rolling a joint,' I told pot connoisseur Roxanne.

'You smoke? I'll wait for you.'

'No, go ahead. I don't smoke. What are your plans for tonight anyway?'

'Nothing. Waiting for you.'

'Oh, do you want to meet somewhere?'

'Why don't you just come over? I'll give you the address.'

'OK,' I said as I reached for a pen. The address he gave was six blocks away. 'I should be there in about twenty minutes.'

'Sure.'

After hanging up I chatted a bit with Roxanne then copied down David's address and phone number at her behest so she'd know where to find my body if he turned out to be a psycho. That's what friends are for. Then I left Roxanne's apartment and wandered up to 49th and 8th.

David, in sweatpants and sweatshirt, opened the door to a clean little one-bedroom. He had just finished his joint and the window was wide open.

'I hope you're not too cold. I'm trying to air out the smoke.'

'No, I'm fine,' I assured, relaxing into the off-white couch. 'I hate the smell of pot smoke so I'd rather have the window open.' David sat next to me.

'You want something to drink? Coffee or something?'

'No, I'm fine,' I repeated contentedly.

David rose to shut the window and get himself some coffee, and then went into the bedroom, returning with a fluffy pillow. 'I knew I forgot something. Here, put it behind your back. It makes the couch more comfortable.'

I thanked him as I took it. With a big comfy cushion and David in pseudo-pj's, I suddenly felt like I was at a slumber party. Luckily, David joined me on the couch coffee in hand to quickly put that notion out of my head.

I took off my shimmering black knee-high boots and David began to massage my legs, making small talk as our bodies got to know one another better. I wondered why he'd been looking at Jimmy the whole time we were chatting at the theatre.

'I wanted to be polite. He's obviously your friend so I wanted to include him in the conversation. But I was looking at you. Actually, I was looking at your tits,' David admitted, laughing self-consciously.

I laughed too, considering my two tits together couldn't fill up one of Pamela Anderson's bra cups. 'Really?'

'Yeah, all natural. That's great!'

It occurred to me that while most guys are dreaming about sex with silicone-enhanced blonde bimbos, strippers probably screwed silicone-enhanced blonde bimbos all the time, desiring the opposite. I was something different. *Au naturel.*

I felt completely at ease with David's powerfully gentle hands caressing my legs, his fingers seeking the black stocking-clad thighs beneath my skirt. There were no pretensions. We both knew what we were there for. All awkwardness disappeared. 'So, you're not bisexual?' I asked.

'Nah,' David replied nonchalantly. 'I only like girls.'

'What type of girls? I mean, besides ones with real tits.'

'Brunettes,' he said without missing a beat.

I shook out my long brown hair. David pulled me closer until I found myself facing him on his lap, my legs wrapped around his torso. 'What's that?' I asked confused as I felt a buzzing radiating from his pocket. I thought it was a beeper.

David shot me a look of wide-eyed mock surprise. 'Toys.'

'You always carry a vibrator in your pocket?'

David laughed heartily. 'I got it when I went into the bedroom to get the pillow.'

Our mouths met, an electric current running from tongue to tongue. 'Did you see me in the audience tonight?' I asked between kisses.

'I saw a shadow of you, but it's hard to see clearly with all the lights onstage.'

'You thought I was a drag queen, huh?'

'No, I didn't think that. But when I saw you by the bathroom the first thing I noticed was your mouth.'

'Really?' I asked surprised. He had just confirmed a pattern I'd spotted only recently. The last few guys I'd been with had fixated on my mouth.

'Yeah. I thought, "That's one perfect, cocksucking mouth",' David explained. I chuckled in appreciation of his honesty so he continued. 'I thought, "I want to try out that mouth. I want to see those lips wrapped around my dick".' David's laughter mingled with my own.

Wow, a man after my own heart, I sighed to myself, relaxing right down to my bones. I'd finally found a guy who shared my no bullshit attitude towards sex. I'd never understood the point of dating – if the sexual chemistry is there why waste time watching a movie when you could get to know one another better in bed? We let our lips linger together a while longer, tasting each other, and then I excused myself to go to the bathroom. Upon my return David directed me to kneel down in front of him.

'Open your mouth.'

'What?' I asked, startled.

'Open your mouth,' David repeated and rubbed his forefinger on my tongue.

'What is that?' I asked, swallowing something salty-sweet.

'It's me.'

'Let me see.'

David tugged down the band of his sweatpants to display his enormous rock-hard dick. 'Suck it.' Enthusiastically I opened wide to caress his cock from shaft to tip in exploration while David guided my journey by yanking my hair. Finally, he brought my head up to stick his fingers between my teeth. 'Suck my fingers.' I obeyed until he took me by the ponytail once again, pushing my mouth back to his ever-expanding hard-on. 'Let me see you. Let me see those lips around my dick,' David commanded, turning my head a bit to the side.

Expertly I varied the rhythm of my tongue until he positioned my head back, asking if I wanted to swallow his cum. 'I don't know you well enough to swallow,' I answered coyly, feeling my power increase as he came closer to losing control.

Snorting like a bull, David suddenly exploded onto my chin, his ejaculate dripping down onto my low neckline. He rubbed his dick across my lips, meeting my eye as he marked his territory with his cum. 'OK. Now I'll take a quick shower and then we'll continue. Do you want a shower, too?' he asked politely as I cleaned his semen from my skin in the kitchen sink.

'No, I'm OK,' I sighed happily, snuggling up on the couch in front of a boring vanilla porno. David's animal-like lack of self-consciousness, his ability to be so at ease in his skin, was contagious. 'This movie's really bad,' I yelled with a yawn as he sauntered into the bathroom.

'Sorry. I just bought it today so I haven't watched it.' David rinsed quickly then returned to the living room, naked and hopping like a jumping bean. 'Cold! Cold! Aren't you freezing?' he asked, trying to shut an already closed window.

'I'm fine,' I shrugged. 'Did you take a cold shower or a hot one?'

'Hot – so now I'm cold.' David grabbed his sweatshirt and put it on. 'That's better.'

I noticed his dick rising again. 'Are you always hard?' I asked, pointing at his growing cock.

'Yeah, I guess so. I can come like, two, three times in a row.'

Definitely a man after my own heart, I thought, as David took a quilt from the bedroom and brought it out to the couch. 'So do you make good money stripping?' I pried.

'Yeah, it's great. I make way more dancing for guys than I ever could for women.'

'You make that much in tips?' I asked dubiously. The crowd that evening didn't seem loaded in the way that the Wall Streeters who frequented the girly clubs were.

'Tips and private sessions,' David stated.

'Do you have to fuck them?'

'Nope, most guys are terrified of AIDS. All you have to do is take off your clothes, let them touch your dick a bit, let them put their mouth on your dick a little bit. That's it.'

'And how much do you make?'

'Two hundred.'

'An hour?'

'No, usually it only takes twenty minutes. Sometimes all you have to do is take off your shirt and they come. Most guys just want to look at you.'

Staring at David's perfectly sculpted form I could definitely understand those johns. 'So what's your favourite thing to do with girls?' I asked, changing the subject. 'Blow jobs?'

After mulling over the question David smiled mischievously. 'I like blow jobs but probably anal sex is my favourite.'

'I've never done it,' I said, the juices between my legs beginning to flow. Anal sex had been a near obsession with me lately, losing my gay boy virginity even more important than popping my pussy's cherry had ever been. This guy seemed to be reading my mind!

'Really? You know the secret, don't you?'

'Uh, you have to have a small dick?' I ventured.

11

'No, size doesn't matter. It's all in the pushing. You have to push down like you're taking a shit.'

'Really?' I asked intrigued. 'Why do you like it so much? Because it's tighter?'

'No – because it makes me completely dominant,' David explained. 'I'm a top.'

Whoa! Had an ex of mine coached this guy? I was ready to propose marriage. 'You like bondage?' I asked hopefully.

'Sure, I like tying up.'

'You like being tied up or tying up?' I clarified, just to double-check I wasn't dreaming.

'Tying up.'

'Well, I love being tied up.' Was it only four years ago that I'd discovered this desire, the need for a psychological orgasm along with the physical? At the time it seemed my whole life had been leading up to the moment when I'd be shackled to a mattress, helpless as a baby, safe in my master's attentive arms. Arthur was a man I had naïvely mistaken for casual sex, a few-months fling, but when he took my S&M virginity by binding me to his bed he tied me forever to his soul as well. I could barely recall the first time I got fucked in the pussy by some Limelight busboy I'd recruited to save me from becoming an old maid at twenty-one – yet instantly I could still conjure up the sound of Arthur's Polish accent, rolling syllables on his tongue like he was tasting a fine wine, setting the rules, telling me no, caring enough to try to tame me. Filling in a missing piece. Never before had I met a man so tender and demanding; over six feet tall with a silky black mane and unrelenting blue eyes. I figured if I could trust him so completely with my body I could trust him with my heart. And then he left me – twice. Once for his future fiancée then again when he died, exactly two years to the day that we'd met.

David nodded. 'Come on,' he said as he got up off the couch and headed towards the bedroom with the pillows and quilt. Like a dog I followed David to the small room where he threw the bedding onto the mattress and began to adjust the lamp. 'You like it like this?'

'A little lower,' I answered as David turned the lights down. After we'd settled into bed I noticed the painting of the Eiffel Tower hanging above our heads. 'Makes you feel more at home?' I kidded.

'This isn't my house! I have no idea why that's up there!' David protested laughing as he took a condom from its wrapper then placed it on the nightstand.

'You always have safe sex?'

'Of course! I like to play – but not with my life.'

After years of dealing with whining condom-phobic men in my serially monogamous life (emphasis on 'serial' – who had time for anything more in New York?), this was refreshing. 'That's very good.'

Our lips met briefly before David shoved my head back between his strong thighs. His cock was gigantic by the time he brought my face up and handed me the condom. 'Put it on.' I obeyed David's command, rolling down inch after throbbing inch with my hungry mouth. Then he flipped me onto my stomach, barking orders as he began to finger and then fuck me. 'No. Put your knees closer together. Down. Lie down!'

I heard him fiddle with a bottle of lube then quickly felt the slippery substance being rubbed inside my pussy – and then inside my ass. David started to probe my asshole; he applied more lube then fingered it again. I was totally astonished and wholly relaxed at the same time. I had given myself over completely to this experienced top. There was no turning back now.

Suddenly, David's massive dick was inside me. 'Push down,' he said softly. 'Push down.' Following orders, I was shocked to find the sex didn't hurt in the least. It all seemed so surreal – as David entered me I simultaneously entered the gay male world; or at least as close as I would ever physically come. Closing my eyes, I happily let my female form slip away.

'Oh, you feel so good,' he whispered in my ear, pinning my arms behind my back. 'Such a good little slave. Now I'm going to come in your ass.' David thrust faster, spanking my butt while paying utmost attention to any signs of pain. If I said 'ouch', he immediately slowed down, holding his breath until I could take more of his thick nine inches.

Finally, his body started to spasm and I heard the cry of a wild beast as David slid his dick from my loosened hole. I wanted to laugh, to scream, to tell the whole world that I had lost my anal virginity! I wanted to bask in the glory of sodomy but suddenly I felt myself turning over and before I knew it, David was hovering above my face, still-hungry hard-on in hand. Tossing aside the used condom, he began to jerk off.

Angry rapping from the other side of the wall startled us back to reality. David waved a friendly hello in the direction of the pissed-off neighbours before commanding me to look at him. I stared at his gorgeous muscular torso only inches away. 'Now pull your hair back.' Not quite comprehending, it took me a second to begin to gather the strands from my face – which wasn't fast enough for David. 'Pull it back! I said to pull it back!'

I rushed to scoop my hair into a ponytail, eyes fixated on his wet dick. 'Now open your mouth. I'm going to come in your face,' he stated tonelessly. I dropped my jaw, half in obedience and half in shock. 'Wider! Open it wider!'

I yawned like I was in the dentist's chair and before I could recover from my astonishment at the situation, David had shot his saved load all over my waiting lips. He smiled down at me, then left the room and returned with a wet washcloth and gently wiped his cum from my skin.

'Wow,' was all I could utter. 'Wow. You are amazing.'

David chuckled. 'I guess that's better than – what was it one girl called me? Awesome! Totally awesome!' David mocked. 'I'll never forget that.'

David went back out to the living room, calling for me to come. I looked at the clock on the nightstand, blinking twenty past two. The whole episode in the bedroom had taken only twenty minutes. Like in a dream, I felt as if I'd been there for hours. I had the urge to be alone in order to process all the information my body had physically consumed.

I joined David and began to get dressed. 'I've got to work in the morning,' I told him, which was true.

'OK,' he nodded understandingly.

He'd complained about how stiff his muscles were so I offered to give him a massage before I left even though I wasn't as good with my hands as I was with my mouth. David directed me through the rubdown as he had through our bedroom sex, after which I wrote my number on a piece of paper and said I'd be his sex slave anytime. We kissed and then I walked out the door, feeling sad that he was leaving me for Atlanta and other men on Monday.

* * *

Two days after losing my ass virginity I arrived home from an easy day of typing and filing for the American Institute of Certified Public Accountants (my part-time gig as an office temp in Jersey City) to find a message from my roommate that David had phoned at noon. Immediately I returned the call, leaving my own starry-tongued message on his machine. My phone rang forty minutes later at twenty to six.

'Hello, baby. How are you?' inquired the French-tinged voice.

'Good, how are you?'

'Tired. I've been working twelve-, fourteen-hour days since I got here.'

'Wow. Did you do any private sessions?'

'Tree today.' It was so cute how he said, 'tree'.

'My, my, Mr Popularity!' I teased.

'Whoa, whoa!' David laughed then paused. 'I just wanted to let you know I'm thinking about the next time I will see you.'

'And when will that be?' I inquired coyly.

'Maybe Saturday. When I get off – around tree in the morning. Are you going out?'

'I haven't decided yet, but even if I do, I can be home by three-thirty.'

'OK. I'll have to get some stuff before I see you.'

'Stuff?'

'I don't know where I can find it but I'll figure it out.'

'You're not going to tell me what kind of stuff?'

'No.'

'It's a secret?'

'Yes.'

'Well, now you've got my curiosity piqued!'

'Good. I have to go do a show now. I'll see you Saturday.'

'I'll be waiting for your call.'

Needless to say, I couldn't wait for Saturday day to be over and done with. I cancelled my plans with Jimmy to save my energy for screwing and was watching a documentary on the Waco siege at eleven when the phone rang. 'Hello, baby. What are you doing home?' David asked.

'I decided to stay in tonight. What are you doing?'

'Looking at toys.'

'Toys?'

'Yeah, I'm trying to figure one out. And I have a tape, too.'

'A tape? Of what?'

'Something for you to watch. Something I think you might enjoy.'

'Oh. What type of toys?'

'I'm not going to tell you.'

'Will you give me a hint?'

'Uh, rubber.'

'Rubber?'

'Yeah.'

'You're trying to figure out something rubber?'

'Yeah, but it comes with a book of directions. I'm reading it right now.'

'Well, you'd better figure it out by three-thirty because I don't want to come over to read a book!' I joked.

'No, I will,' he assured. 'I'll call you when I get off of work, baby.'

Of course, by the time 'tree'-thirty rolled around, I was wide awake and counting the minutes. When the phone rang at exactly quarter to four I leapt to the receiver. 'You want me to come over now?' I asked hopefully after exchanging greetings.

'Yes.'

'OK. If I leave now I should make it up there in fifteen or twenty minutes.' After hanging up I grabbed my purse and coat and zoomed out the door. By the time the cab reached 49th Street my stomach was turning, my heart pounding. I remembered something I was taught in acting school – about how people hate to feel nervous and love to feel excited even though nervousness and excitement are physiologically really just the same thing. I was utterly thrilled and completely scared to death.

I rang the apartment and was promptly buzzed in through the double doors. I made my way up to the second floor where David greeted me shirtless and in jeans and sneakers, his powerful tanned muscles beckoning me to come inside. His body screamed 'porn star' as he quietly shut the door behind me and sat down on the couch. With legs wide open and relaxed he took a sip of diet Pepsi then a drag off his cigarette as he studied me taking off my coat. 'Come over here.' I walked over to him, feeling extremely self-conscious under his stare. 'Turn around.' Slowly I did as I was told and David ran his hands down my body, inspecting the small tight black top and white PVC skirt I had chosen carefully. As I came full-circle to face him he brought me to my knees to meet his lips.

'You like the outfit? I tried to think of what you might like,' I stammered. 'The skirt's submissive.'

David nodded knowingly, a big grin on his face. 'This body can wear anything.' I laughed in relief and David kissed me again. Then he pushed me back onto my feet. 'Stand up. Turn around. Bend over and lift up your skirt. I want to see your ass.' I obeyed and he began to caress my butt and legs lightly. 'Very good. Now go to the bathroom and take off your panties and bra. Everything else stays on.'

I left the living room, got undressed and dressed again then returned to where David stood holding out his hand. I deposited my sheer black panties and Victoria's Secret bra into his palm. He sniffed then threw them aside. Then he pointed me back to the couch.

I sat down, watching David curiously as he went to the bathroom and came back with a long white towel. My curiosity, though, turned to horror when he nonchalantly retrieved a huge serrated silver knife from the kitchen. Holding both up to me in full view he used the knife to split the towel in two. 'You know what this is for?' he asked, displaying the shreds. Too terrified to speak, I shook my head though I knew the answer. 'You'll see,' David said as he put the knife and two pieces on the small table by the couch. 'Now stand up. I want everything off but your top.'

I obeyed my master. Impulsively I decided I would be the best little slave in the world for David. I craved the ego trip inherent in garnering praise from this living gay male fantasy before me, to be the desired object of an object of desire. When I was naked save for my tight black blouse David came over with a towel shred and secured my arms behind my back. Then he walked around to face me, taking both my breasts in his hands to vulnerably hang them over the neckline of my top. I had no clue as to what he was thinking since by now I was afraid to read his gaze. With my head down, I simply stared at my feet. A pillow hit the floor in front of me.

'Get down on your knees,' David commanded, in the same tone he had been using all night. By now I felt more threatened by his voice than by anything he was actually doing to me. Not once had he raised it. He simply spoke to me in the firm way one would

19

speak to a dog in obedience school. *You will do what I say. I don't have to raise my voice because I am in control and you have no other choice.*

I knelt on the pillow as David turned down the lights. My heart beat wildly with a strange mix of fear and invincibility. He came up behind me, shook the smaller piece of towel in front of my face then proceeded to blindfold me with it. This was too much too soon. Panic set in. 'Mercy. No. No blindfold, please,' I stuttered. Fortunately, David respected my wishes and I relaxed. Circling slowly around my body, he removed the belt from his pants. Hovering in front of me, he began to strap it around my neck. Uh-oh.

I felt horrible about being such a bad slave but a strap around my throat trumped even a blindfold! I was shocked speechless. Luckily, David spoke for me.

'Do you have anything to say before we begin?' he asked softly as the buckle started to slink its way towards my bare neck. It sounded like he was asking if I had any last requests before dying.

'Yes – yes,' I stammered. 'I – I don't like belts. Do you want my collar? It's in my purse.'

'You have a collar?'

'Yeah, go into my purse,' I whispered.

David opened my bag and found my bondage gear. 'You have chains for these?' he inquired, flashing my restraints. I shook my head as David returned to where I knelt, trading his belt for my collar, which he fastened around my neck – too tightly.

'Will you loosen it please?' I was being a terrible slave, but considering we had neglected to discuss my limits beforehand – a big S&M no-no! – I felt I was within bounds to voice concern. (Thanks to the year I'd spent answering phones for Arena/Blaze, one of

NYC's top dungeons, I knew the rules of safe play better than the Ten Commandments!)

After adjusting my collar, David used it to bring me to my feet. 'Bend over.' He rubbed my smooth butt in preparation of his spanking. I whimpered in sync with the whacks, feeling like a guinea pig in some strange sadomasochistic experiment, David testing my pliability and resilience. I stood shaking as I heard him rummage through a plastic bag then felt the touch of rubber strips on the backs of my thighs. It wasn't until I recognised the sound of a cat o' nine tails on bare ass that I realised I was being whipped. I held my breath, my desire to be transformed from female to object overcoming my low tolerance for pain. David alternated the flogging with the caress of his palm with the paddling of his hand and I knew he was going to leave marks and bruises. And yet I didn't say a word – not even when I felt his teeth bite the skin of my ass. I'd become as still as a marble statue, raw material for my master's strong hands.

An eternity passed before David unbound my wrists. He stood me up, lit a cigarette and inhaled deeply, then dropped onto the couch and plopped a pillow on the floor between his wide-open legs. Calmly, he took a sip of diet Pepsi. 'Kneel down,' David commanded matter-of-factly and I obeyed. 'Take off my shoes.'

I obeyed.

'Socks.'

I obeyed.

'Take off my pants.' I obeyed until David was more naked than I was. He reached for the bottle of lube on the table by the couch, and squirted a generous amount onto his cock. 'Take your rings off. Rub my dick with your hands,' he continued after I'd removed

21

the jewellery. My fingers slipped and slid over David's hard-on, following the directions he was giving. He raised his voice to a level of severity only if I didn't comply the first time he discharged an order.

'Slowly. I said slowly!' David's cock had grown to the proportion he was paid for when he rose from the couch and walked over to the plastic bag on the kitchen table. 'OK. Sit down on the couch and watch your movie.'

I had completely forgotten the video David had bought me – a bondage porno – playing silently the entire time. Or maybe I had just shut the sound off in my head, so focused was I on David's voice. I couldn't tell.

David left for the bathroom then returned with another towel, setting it on the floor in front of the couch. He went back again. When I heard the dim buzzing noise thoughts of *The Texas Chainsaw Massacre* scrambled through my brain.

'OK, get up,' David ordered, suddenly appearing with a small black object in his hand. He took my place on the couch as I stood on the towel facing away and brushed the buzzing thing over my buttocks. As metal met skin I realised he was shaving the fine hair there. An unexpected calm swept over me like a surprise wave – the clutter in my head, all human thoughts and emotions, dragged away with each stroke of the electric razor like seashells returning with the tide. 'OK, bend over.' The ritual of removal continued until he had stripped me naked from pussy to ass. My mind transformed into an empty beach, a blank canvas for David's desires.

He rose to retrieve a washcloth. 'Much better. Now clean yourself off in the bathroom with soap and water,' he commanded, handing me the dry cloth.

Hunched over in the tub, water running over my newly exposed pussy and ass, I soon felt embarrassed and ashamed, like a bad little girl. 'Come here,' David said from his place on the couch as I tentatively approached minutes later. I settled between his strong thighs and David explored my mouth with his tongue while admiring his shaving work with his hands. I wanted to slip beneath his skin, feel the blood rush that my bare pussy was causing. After dribbling lube on his fingers he harshly pried inside me, front and back. 'Give me your tongue.' Uncomprehending, I simply continued my French kiss. 'No – I said to give me your tongue! Stick it out! All the way!'

Inhaling my tongue, David bit down then released it to push me to my shaky knees. 'Open your mouth – wide!' Our combined saliva descended from David's lips to mine and I swallowed instinctively. I gasped for air and he turned me away. The bag from the kitchen table was now at his side and I could hear him take something from it.

A phallus, cold and slippery, entered me, first in my pussy then another in my ass. I concentrated on David's breathing, narcissistically measuring my hold over his erection with each heavy sigh. Even after hearing the snaps of the little leather straps around my thighs securing the plugs into place I hadn't a clue as to what I was wearing. All I knew was that it wasn't very comfortable – especially in my tight asshole. I remembered David's voice telling me to push down as I relaxed into the violating object. His groan of pleasure made me hungry for more.

Another buzzing sounded and the device began pulsating inside me. I had the strange sensation of being a remote-controlled toy as David played with the different 'gears' of the contraption, forcing the vibrations faster then slower, thoroughly enjoying his new porn star Barbie doll. I basked in my new-found sexual perfection, my ability to give so much pleasure the ultimate power trip. When he tired of playing, David switched me off then positioned me kneeling on the couch, face to the wall.

'Beautiful – that looks beautiful! You are such a good machine!' David exclaimed like Dr Frankenstein complimenting his perfect creation. 'Go into the bedroom. Take off your top,' he continued after unplugging me.

Once I'd set my tight shirt on the nightstand I stood obediently beside the bed to wait for my master. 'Come onto the bed. Mouth. Put my dick in your mouth,' David ordered tonelessly as he took a seat on the mattress. Running my tongue down his thick shaft, tasting his sweet erection, I winced as David played with then twisted my nipples, testing my threshold for both pleasure and pain. All that kept me from crying out when he slapped my left breast was the tip of his dick on my tonsils. 'Here, roll it on with your mouth,' David directed, offering me a condom. Slowly and carefully my lips ran the latex along his shaft. After double-checking my novice work to ensure the rubber was secure, David thrust his erection into my wet open pussy as I sat on his lap, thighs wrapped around his waist.

'Can I go to the bathroom, please?' I pleaded. The position was hell on my bladder. Permission granted, I rushed to pee then returned to climb back onto the bed but David stopped me.

'Where do you think you're going? Get on the floor. On your knees.'

Mouth open wide, I accepted David's massive cock, my knees sinking into the pillow he'd placed on the carpet. Playfully I ran my tongue along the shaft, teasing the tip then hungrily taking inch after inch down my throat, horny with his pleasure. Groaning, David brought me onto the bed to position me on my back on top of his six-pack abs. His fat dick slid in and out of my pussy as his slick fingers probed my asshole until I soon felt something bigger than a finger in my loosening hole. He pushed me up and onto my stomach then continued to fuck me from behind, his hard-on pounding away the remnants of my ass virginity. I started to feel pain, begged him to slow down, then listened while he held his breath in anticipation. When I felt I could handle more I whispered, 'Do you like it in there? Do you like fucking my ass?'

David could control himself no longer. I moaned softly as he conquered my body. 'Use me. I just want to be your toy. I want to be used.' The words floated above me, disembodied. I existed only to please him. I was a mere vessel for his wildest dreams.

David pulled out and removed his condom. 'Up – get up and suck me.'

I dropped onto my knees and worshipped his engorged cock with my tongue, varying my rhythm with his caveman grunts. Grabbing my hair to steal the music from my mouth, he released himself all over my face, convulsing with a roar. He held my head tight until the last drop of cum had dripped from my satisfied lips.

He went to the bathroom to wash up. When he returned I followed him into the living room. We lay exhausted on the couch watching the movie *Se7en*, and it wasn't until David rose to search for his cigarettes that I noticed something wasn't right.

'Is this in French?'

'What?'

'This movie! Brad Pitt's speaking French.'

'So?'

'So Brad Pitt doesn't speak French!'

'Yeah, but I speak French.'

'Yeah, but this is an American movie. You don't see me renting Truffault or Godard films where everyone speaks English. Did Morgan Freeman just say *excusez-moi*? Oh, shit! This is hysterical!'

I went into a laughing fit that I couldn't stop. *Se7en* in French was akin to a great Monty Python sketch! David stared at me like I was crazy but pretty soon my giggles grew so contagious that he choked on the water he was drinking, causing a coughing fit to rival my laughing one. After catching our breaths we returned to the bedroom where I offered David a massage before bed.

'Your muscles are so tight,' I noted, my palms forming circles along his shoulder blades. 'How many sessions did you do today? Three?'

'Six.'

'Wow – all that work and then you come home and dominate me? Poor thing!'

'Yeah, but you're like my dessert after dealing with faggots all day.'

'What did you think about during your sessions?'

'What do you think? I spent the whole day shopping for toys in between sessions. I was hard all day long!'

'So I guess I made you money.'

'Yeah.'

I caressed David's neck until he started to doze off. 'Wait!'

'What?'

'*Se7en* is still on.'

26

'What?'

'You left the movie on. I can hear Brad Pitt speaking French.'

'So?'

'I can't sleep if Brad Pitt is speaking French!'

'You've got to be kidding me!'

'No, I'm serious. Turn it off!' I begged. Grumpily, David went to the living room to shut up Brad Pitt. Then we both slept soundly until the alarm rang at one the following afternoon. He had a session at one-thirty. 'I wish I was your client,' I sighed, rushing to dress.

'No, you don't. I have no time for my clients. It's like "OK, we're done, gotta go".'

'Well, I still wish I could see you for a session,' I teased. I wondered if the chemistry he had with his clients was like ours. For me, sex stripped down to its bare animal essence was a liberation of the soul.

'I get off work at midnight tonight,' he stated slyly. 'Maybe then?'

'OK.'

'I'll call you tonight, baby.'

We kissed goodbye and I walked out the door, my butt a bit bruised but my soul in total bliss.

It was half past midnight when I called David from a phone booth in the downstairs lobby of the Directors Guild Theater at 57th and 6th. I'd been taking advantage of the free Russian Film Festival pass Roxanne had given me and had just witnessed what was undoubtedly the most bizarre screening of my life. 'This Russian film by Sokurov about Adolf Hitler and Eva Braun that was shot in German, dubbed into Russian for the festival, and then simultaneously translated live into English,' I gushed in answer to David's question as to what movie I'd seen.

'Whoa! Whoa! Slow down! I just smoked a joint and I asked you what movie you saw and you throw all these names at me.'

'Sorry. *Molokh* – it's called *Molokh*.'

'That's what I asked.'

'So do you want me to come over?' I eagerly inquired.

'Yes, I'm really hungry, though. I just got off of work. You want to go get something to eat? McDonald's?'

'Yuck, I don't eat meat but I'm not really hungry. I'll go with you, though, if you can wait ten minutes.'

'I can wait ten minutes.'

'I'm leaving now.' I walked briskly downtown to David's apartment and rang the buzzer. He came downstairs and greeted me with a smile and a kiss. As we headed towards Times Square I briefed him on the surreal dubbing experience I'd just sat through. 'It was worse than *Se7en*!' David laughed uproariously. Finally arriving at the giant Mardi Gras-lit McDonald's in the heart of New Disneyland, David ordered a burger and fries while I found an empty table for us upstairs. While he ate, his eyes bored into me. 'What?' I asked, feeling incredibly self-conscious.

'Nothing.' He shook his head then flashed a naughty smile. 'I'm hard right now.'

'You're kidding me!' I chuckled, flattered. 'That's very sexy, though. Were you hard all day?'

'Mmm-hmm. I even came on the floor at work.'

I laughed in surprise. 'You're not supposed to do that – are you?'

'No, no – of course not! But I came backstage and I started flipping through a porno and – you know, you have like two minutes to get hard and then you

28

have to go back onstage – and I was trying to get hard and all of a sudden I see this picture of a girl getting whipped. I couldn't stop. I mean, I didn't want to stop. So I went too far and came all over the floor. And my friend, another dancer who is talking with a couple other guys backstage, looks over and he says, "What the *hell* are you doing?"'

'He asked you what the hell you were doing?' I repeated between giggles.

'Yeah, yeah. I just said I couldn't stop.'

'That's hysterical!'

'So,' David asked as he finished his meal, 'what do you like to do – besides fuck and go to movies?'

'Hmm. Well, I like to write and direct movies – short films right now – and I like to kickbox and go dancing. In terms of sports, I guess kickboxing, dancing and fucking are my favourites.'

'That's good.' David smiled warmly. 'You want some dessert? I want ice cream.'

'Really? It's freezing outside! No, thanks.'

'So, you don't eat meat, huh?' he asked as we waited in line for his artificial vanilla goop.

'Not if it's dead,' I said slyly. 'Oh, by the way, I have to show you the artwork you left on my body.'

'What?'

'You left some artwork on my butt.' David grinned smugly, obviously pleased as we exited the garish Golden Arches. He was happily spooning ice cream into his mouth when an older blond businessman in glasses and tie appeared walking towards us. When David waved unabashedly the guy smiled uncomfortably. 'Client?' I asked once the guy had passed.

'Yeah, I just saw him today.'

'Well, he seemed pretty freaked out when he saw me. What – does he think you're gay?'

'No, no – my clients know. Oh, please, he's not freaked out – he's getting off on it! He's thinking, "Ah, there's this guy with his girlfriend and I had him only a few hours before!" Oh, wait! I want to go in here,' David said, stopping in front of an adult video store. 'Come on.' I followed David into the fluorescent-lit shop. 'You have *Se7en*?' he asked the clerk.

'Do I have what?' It was past one in the morning and the Indian salesman was obviously expecting this couple to be looking for something hotter than Morgan Freeman.

'*Se7en*.'

'The regular movie?'

'Yeah, with Brad Pitt. Do you have it?' David tried again impatiently.

'Uh, no,' the guy answered quite confused. As we left I asked David why he wanted *Se7en* if he already had it in French.

'Because you can't watch it.'

'Well, actually I *can* watch it. I just watch the comedy version. Why do we have to watch *Se7en* anyway? Is it your favourite movie?'

'Well, not exactly. It's just – it puts me to sleep.'

'What?' I asked, as confused as the clerk.

'It's like a sleeping pill for me.'

'You're joking! It's a thriller – it's supposed to do the opposite!'

'I don't know what it is but I turn that movie on and – boom! I'm out like a light.'

'That is so weird,' I said laughing. 'It's a good thing they didn't use you for their advertising campaign.'

David fished his apartment key from his jeans pocket as we drifted west on 49th Street. Once inside the cosy pad on the second floor I offered David a massage while he finished his dessert. He nodded with a mouthful of McGoop. As I sat on the couch with David shirtless atop a pillow on the floor between my legs I stared at his gorgeous wings tattooed from shoulder blade to lower back. I caressed every feather, willing my fingers to memorise his skin as he sighed heavily, whispering praises to me in French.

'I love serving you,' I uttered softly in his ear. He reached up to bring my head towards his mouth and gently bit my lip.

'Hand me my cigarettes,' he stated as the taste of vanilla lingered on my lips. I rubbed his tight shoulders while he smoked. When he was through he rose from the floor, ordering me into the bedroom. 'Take the pillow with you and take off your clothes.'

I did, then lay face down on the mattress, so as to proudly display the light purple bruises and whip marks he'd left on my ass. Moments later, David appeared in the doorway, naked and hard, and walked over to run his hands gently over my buttocks. He smiled broadly before turning me over.

'That looks good but something's missing,' he said as he forced a finger inside my pussy.

'What?'

'Something's missing. Hmm, I know. A piercing.'

'What?'

'You need a clit piercing.'

'I do?'

'Uh-huh. So I can play with it.'

'OK,' I said uncertainly. 'Anything else?'

'No, that's it for now,' he answered as he climbed on top of me. He threw my legs over my head, prying my pussy open with his tongue. 'Spread your lips apart. Spread them! Use your hands!' David commanded. I submitted to his hungry mouth until he switched positions to hover above me, his fat cock in my face. 'Open your mouth.' Eagerly I worshipped David's dick, tonguing the wet tip, anxious to please, to tease his huge balls until his desire turned to other holes. 'Get a condom,' he ordered, pushing me away.

I reached over to where he usually kept one on the nightstand but grasped air. 'Where are they?' I asked breathlessly.

'You don't have any?'

'No, of course not – you always have some here.'

'Yeah, but I used them all. Oh, shit.' David left and began searching the bathroom. 'Shit! And I really wanted to fuck you. OK,' he sighed in resignation upon returning to the room. 'I'm going to come in your face instead. Get off the bed – on your knees on the floor. Open your mouth.'

David towered above me, holding his engorged cock with the care reserved for a loaded gun. With his left hand he yanked my head back by the hair while my lids instinctively fluttered shut. 'No – look at me! Look at me! Open your eyes!' David ordered slowly and firmly. Menacingly he stared me down as he jerked his slick dick with a vengeance. 'Open your mouth. I'm going to come in your face. You want that?'

'Whatever you want,' I whispered overwhelmed.

'What? I can't hear you!'

'Whatever you want,' I replied, regaining my voice.

'Wider! I want that mouth open wider! That's it! That's it! Yes! Grrrahhh!' His body convulsed like an epileptic having a minor seizure. Recovering, David used my face to wipe his dick, spreading the dripping cum over my cheeks and onto my lips. Then he released my hair and went into the bathroom. 'You are a very good slave.'

When David returned I left to wash up. When I got back he was trying to figure out the alarm clock. 'What time do you want it set for?' he inquired.

'I have to be at work by noon. Nine or nine-thirty is fine. What time do you leave for Atlanta?'

'Twelve-thirty.'

'It's good you're leaving tomorrow,' I said.

'Why?'

'Because then I'll have something to look forward to. When will you be back?'

'Beginning of February.'

'Call me before you come in and let me know what I should do to prepare for your visit.'

'Yes,' David answered as we both crawled into bed and promptly fell asleep.

Awaking before the alarm rang I switched it off so it wouldn't disturb my master. Then I dressed, finally waving my hand in front of David's peaceful face until his eyes gradually opened. He looked up at me, pointing at his lips. I kissed him goodbye.

'I'll see you in February,' I said as I left him still half asleep with his dreams. Then I walked out the door and back into my life, his smell on my skin, the piece of male soul I'd stolen tucked away deep inside.

The Return of Sir David

(February 2000)

So when I got David's message that first day of February I wasted no time, immediately grabbing the phone to dial the number he had left. He answered on the first ring. 'Hey, David –'

'Hey!' he happily interrupted.

'It's Lauren,' I continued pointlessly. 'I've been waiting for your call all week.'

'Well, I just got into town yesterday.'

'Working hard?'

'Yup, I just finished with a client. Did you just get home from work?'

'Yeah, like two minutes ago.'

'What are you doing tonight?'

'Going to the gym in a couple hours – other than that nothing.'

'Going to the gym? Getting that tight ass even tighter?'

'What? I can't understand what you're saying.' The French accent again.

David repeated his flirtation and I laughed. 'Yeah, I guess so.'

'Mmmm,' David growled. 'I'm getting hard right now.'

'Just from talking to me?'

'Yup.'

'That's what I like to hear!' I exclaimed, flattered. 'So what are you doing tonight? You have to work, right?'

'Till midnight.'

'You want to see me then?'

'Yes. Are you shaved?'

'Uh, no. Is that bad?'

'No, it's OK. I prefer to do it myself.'

'What should I wear?'

David pondered the question like a game show contestant in the final round. 'Something – slave-like – latex –'

'Shit! I don't have latex. You didn't give me any warning,' I reminded. 'PVC?'

'That's OK. We can get latex tomorrow,' he assured me. 'PVC is fine.'

'Um, is a red PVC skirt and black PVC top OK?' I asked hesitantly.

'Yes, wear that. And socks –'

'Stockings you mean?'

'Yes – and shoes with heels.'

I felt like we were planning for a fashion shoot. 'Anything else?'

'No, that's good. I'll call you tonight.'

Luckily I had my kickboxing class to rush off to and expel all my nervous energy. I relaxed, basking in endorphins for a bit, but as the clock ticked towards midnight the leather collar around my neck began to tighten. The phone rang at five to twelve.

'Hey, baby.'

'Hey!'

'Listen – I have a client. I'll need another twenty, twenty-five minutes.'

'No problem. Call me when you're done,' I said understandingly. As I hung up the phone I flashed back to my dungeon management days at Arena/ Blaze when I would have to inform various spouses and significant others that their wives or girlfriends still had twenty minutes of spanking and cock and ball torture to go – and would they mind waiting? I felt like I was dating a dominatrix. 'All done?' I inquired when David phoned again thirty-five minutes later.

'Yeah. The guy came too soon so I talked to him for a while.'

'That's nice.'

'I just need to go to McDonald's.'

'OK. If I leave in ten minutes will that be enough time?'

'Perfect.'

I finished the transsexual-on-the-run-road-adventure novel I was reading then threw on my faux fur coat. With all the snow and ice on the sidewalk there was no way I'd be wearing my black six-inch fetish platforms outside. Instead I tossed them in my purse along with my wrist restraints and a couple of condoms then slipped into my sparkly black knee-high boots.

It was freezing outside so I quickly hailed a cab. I made sure my coat was buttoned to the top to hide my leather collar as I paid the driver then walked into the lobby of the hotel on 46th Street – right up the block from where I once worked as a receptionist at a body rub place before it was shuttered and three girls arrested as part of Giuliani's quality-of-life crusade. That's when I got my safely-in-the-grey-legal-area job at a house of domination.

The desk clerk was busy assisting a buff blond stripper so he only gave me a brief accusatory glance as I sauntered to the elevator, looking like a call girl. Young things in tart red lipstick and knee-high boots don't just wander into Times Square hotels at one on a Tuesday morning unless they were 'ordered'. In a way, I guess I was. It was just that the hustler was the one doing the 'ordering'. As I passed, the boy toy did a hungry double-take, confirming my guess he was 'gay for pay'.

Not desiring to draw any more attention to myself by searching for the stairs, I took the elevator to the second floor where I fortunately found David's room right away and rapped lightly on the door. He answered exactly how I thought he would – shirtless and wearing only jeans and sneakers, a proud display of tanned blue-collar muscle. His smile met my lips before he took a seat at the little wooden desk. As he started to roll a cigarette, I remained in the doorway still clutching the top of my coat. 'Now, before I take this off I have to tell you that the outfit isn't all that submissive,' I announced.

'Let me see,' David commanded, prompting with his hand.

Self-consciously I stood in front of him, PVC pressed tight against my skin. He nodded mysteriously. 'I look like a dominatrix, don't I?' I apologised.

'No. It's OK. Come closer,' he said softly, patting his leg.

'I used to work a block away from here – answering phones at a body rub place,' I confessed, sitting like a nervous little girl on Santa's lap. 'Small world.' In mute concentration David continued his enigmatic nodding, sealing tobacco in white paper. 'My sister was at the Gaiety a couple weeks ago. She said all the strippers were really ugly. Are they?'

'Well, I don't know. I wasn't here two weeks ago.'

'No, I mean this week. Are they cute?'

'Two or tree,' David answered uninterested as he tapped a little red object into one end of the handmade cancer stick.

'What's that?'

'A filter – what do you think?'

'I don't know. Americans don't roll their own cigarettes!' My small talk definitely wasn't cutting it. 'So did you miss my mouth or my ass more?' I tried.

Lighting up as he carefully pondered the question, David finally replied, 'Both.'

'Really?'

He mulled it over again, his eyes scanning my tight outfit. 'Actually, everything.'

'Really? You're not lying?' I asked too anxiously.

'Nope.'

'Good! I just want to please you. You make me so nervous.'

David set down his cigarette and began stroking my thigh. 'Open your mouth. Wider,' he continued, inspecting my throat like a doctor. 'That is *the* most perfect cocksucking mouth!' he declared. I smiled as he ran his hand up and down my body, stroked my skin then sniffed it. Like a curious dog he inhaled the perfumed scent of my biceps, my armpits, then tugged at my top to see what lay beneath.

'I'm wearing a bra to match the skirt.'

'Show me.' I slipped out of the PVC, revealing a red bra with black leopard spots fit for a slut. 'I don't like it,' David stated matter-of-factly.

'But I colour coordinated!' I whined.

'Take it off. Leave the black top on.' As I did, David held me close against his crotch, the bulge inside his jeans growing to get out. 'So, has anyone played with your ass since I last saw you?'

Was that a trick question? We'd never discussed other partners. Going by my 'honesty is the best policy' I replied, 'No, but he tried.'

'Couldn't do it, though?' David inquired mockingly, wagging his finger and shaking his head in faux shame. 'Stand up,' he ordered, pushing me from his lap. 'You're not shaved, right?'

'No.'

'Take off your stockings and panties and bend over on the floor.' Quickly I obeyed as David left for the bathroom. I heard a buzzing noise before he returned to where I kneeled on all fours. 'Look at that! You're not shaved at all! What's the matter with you? Can't I trust you to keep yourself clean?' Startled speechless I simply stared at my 'paws'. 'What? I can't hear you!'

'S-sorry,' I stammered.

'Sorry what? You're to say "sorry, master".'

'Sorry, master. Sorry, sir.'

'That's better. Now this is the last time I do this for you!' I held still as the electric razor cleared a path along the crack of my ass. 'Stand up. Foot up. Put your foot up on the bed,' David directed, gently gliding the buzzing blade over my pussy. 'OK, down on your knees. Give me your mouth.' Marking his territory, David spat on my lips then smeared the saliva over my cheeks with his tongue. 'You're going to suck my cock now. Take off my shoes and pants.' With my face feeling slimy I pulled at David's heavy sneakers then undid the fly of his jeans and removed them as well. I stared at the skintight red briefs, the outline of hard-on through cloth. A circle of pre-cum seeped through the red. 'Look what you made me do!' David admonished.

'Sorry, sir.'

After tugging off the stained underwear David grabbed the back of my head, forcing my face onto the wet spot on his belly. 'Lick it off!' he barked.

I lapped at his steel stomach until he shoved my head to his hard dick. I'd forgotten the enormity of David's cock until I felt the tip gagging the back of my throat and realised I hadn't even gotten half in my mouth. I wrapped my right hand around the shaft in a futile attempt to gain control, slowly tonguing my way to his ecstasy until David stopped me. Cupping my face in his palms he leaned down, staring deep into my eyes. 'I almost came in your mouth,' he said threateningly, then pushed my head away. 'Sit down on the bed,' he ordered as he arranged the pillows in a pile in the middle before methodically checking the set-up from different angles like a pornographic cinematographer. *What next – a light reading?* I wondered as David took his sweet time adjusting the fluffy cushions.

'So, why are you staying in a hotel this time?' I asked, trying the small talk route again.

Ignoring me, David continued to concentrate on his cushion arranging. 'OK. Lie face down on the pillows,' he finally announced. 'Fucking slut. I'm going to fuck that ass,' he muttered to himself, standing behind where I lay. He hiked up my skirt, penetrated me anally with a finger then leaned down close to my ear. 'You'd better be good,' he warned before instantly swinging my legs around so they hung limply off the bed. The finger in my ass invaded further, forcing cold lube deeper and deeper inside me. 'Spread those cheeks! Use your hands!' David ordered. As I grabbed the two firm mounds of flesh, prying apart my butt cheeks, David popped his finger from my hole to watch the show. 'Hello!' he cried happily. 'I remember you!' he told my ass. I wished I'd gotten as warm a greeting as my asshole did.

With expert fingers David loosened both my tight holes. I struggled to keep my own hands from sliding off my lube-drenched butt cheeks but when I felt David's cock enter me anally I simply gave up. He was thrusting so hard that when he pulled out and turned me over to throw my legs uncomfortably over my head I was overjoyed for the break. I wondered how much more my novice asshole could take.

And I was soon to find out. With my pussy wet in preparation, I was quite shocked when David rammed his fat hard-on back inside my ass while still holding my legs firmly in the air. I pondered how much longer it would be before I cried 'mercy'. Fortunately, David decided to save his orgasm, pulling out to remove his condom and take a seat on a nearby chair. 'Over here – on your knees. You're going to suck my cock again for a while.' Eagerly I took his thick dick between my lips. 'No! Not so rough! Slower!'

As I ran my tongue seductively along the shaft, his cock grew even bigger. A latex aftertaste wetted my appetite and I was forced to use my hands to keep from gagging on the gigantic muscle. David immediately pushed them away, plunging even deeper. I was sure I was going to choke.

'What's the matter with you? Can't suck my cock right? You'd better or I'll fuck you in the ass again. Is that what you want?'

'No, sir,' I gurgled.

'Then suck!' But the enormity of it was just too much for my aching throat. David yanked me off his disappointed dick harshly by the hair. 'OK, this is what we're gonna do,' he stated calmly. 'I'm gonna fuck that mouth and then if you can't do that you're gonna take it up the ass.' Controlling his rhythm with a firm right hand at the back of my head, David wielded his dick like a drill, hoping to strike gold. Desperately I tried to use my hands again but it was like orally riding a bronco. 'That's it. No good,' he finally declared in exasperation. 'Here's a condom. Roll it on with your mouth. Now stand up!' he commanded after I'd slid the rubber along his shaft with quaking lips. 'No more chances for you. Turn around. Sit down.' Following orders I lowered myself onto his slick cock until I felt the round head penetrate my tight asshole. 'You feel that?' he whispered in my ear as his dick delved deeper inside. 'Feel the difference?'

'Yes, it hurts.'

'What?'

'It hurts.' Disgusted by my poor behaviour, David pushed me prone onto the mattress and rammed me anally harder and faster in frustration. 'Mercy!' I finally cried, prompting David to pull out and flip me onto my back.

'I'm going to come all over you! You want that?' he threatened.

'Whatever you want, sir,' I whispered, not realising that when he said he was going to 'come all over me' he was being literal. After removing his second condom of the night, David jerked on the huge erection until a virtual volcano erupted. He cried out like a rabid animal as semen spurted all over my stomach, chest, face and hair. Then he collapsed on top of me like a fallen tree. I lay completely still, soaked in cum and amazed. When he rose to shower I ran my fingers through the sticky wads in my hair. 'You came in my hair,' I told him when he returned to the room.

'I came everywhere!' he laughed.

'Yeah, the maid's not going to be too happy with you in the morning. I wonder if cum works as a conditioner.'

David laughed even harder as he towelled off. 'I have no idea.'

I got up and went into the bathroom while David readied for bed. 'You want a massage before I go?' I asked once I was dressed.

'Oh, yeah!' David enthused then belly-flopped onto the bed. Like an explorer I climbed on top of his buff body, rubbing the ridges of rock hard biceps, caressing the crevices of tattooed shoulder blades. *Hello! I remember you!*

David murmured appreciatively.

'So do you always have to think of girls when your clients suck you off?' I asked curiously.

'No. If they're good I don't have to think of anything. There are certain things I like doing with guys. I consider myself maybe ten percent gay.'

'Really?' I said happily surprised. 'Well, I consider myself a gay boy. Inside at least,' I continued, blowing my covert status.

David craned his neck, shooting me a look that asked, *'What on earth are you talking about?'* Was I revealing too much?

'Yeah,' I continued. 'I mean, I'm a woman on the outside and a gay boy on the inside. I think like a guy,' I explained. 'If I had a dime for every guy I've been with who's told me he's never met anyone like me I'd be able to quit my job!' David laughed lightheartedly so I began to reveal more. 'That's why it's nice being with you. You don't think I'm weird because you're used to being with guys. Most straight guys aren't cool with girls with boys' brains.' As my hands squeezed the tension from the two perfect globes below his back David purred in pleasure. 'So what else do you like to do with guys besides getting sucked off?' I inquired.

'That's it.'

'What?' I said disappointed.

'That's it. Nothing else.'

'Well, that's not a very gay answer. That's pretty straight.'

'Sorry,' David chuckled. After finishing the massage I rose to get my coat. As I zipped up my sweatshirt and threw my hood over my head David turned over and beamed up at me.

'I hope I didn't forget anything.'

'Don't worry. You'll be back.'

I kissed my master goodbye and drifted dreamily out the door. Hailing a cab on 6th I couldn't help but think how much more of a cocksucker I was than my 'ten percent gay' hustler.

Three days passed without a phone call from my master. To say I was on edge was an understatement. I was a wreck inside. What did I do wrong? Had he found someone else to dominate? Why hadn't he called? On Saturday I cried mercy and left a message at his hotel. 'Hey, David. It's Lauren,' I said breezily. 'Just checking to see if we're getting together again before you leave so give me a call. Bye.' Then I went shopping with Jimmy for a cobalt-blue shirt for him and new boots for me. We were going to another 'straight-friendly' gay Latin club, 'La Nueva Escuelita', on 39th Street that evening and I swore to Jimmy I'd be wearing my lucky red dress with a vengeance if David didn't call.

I returned home two hours later, thrilled with my purchase of black stretch glitter boots for ten bucks at Joyce Leslie. Even better, the message light was blinking on my answering machine. I hit the button and held my breath.

'Hey, baby,' sighed the tired French accent from the machine. 'Still working, working, working. If you want to see me I get off work at tree so – I didn't call yesterday because it got too late – but call me, leave a message if you want to see me between tree and four so we can play a little – and then sleep. Let me know, baby.'

Of course, I called back immediately. 'Hey, David,' I greeted his machine. 'I would love to see you between three and four. I'm actually going dancing at a club about ten blocks away from you. I can call you from the club around three-thirty if you want. Just call me back and let me know what you want me to do.' Then I phoned Roxanne to tell her about the sexy new boots and to play her the sexy new voice.

'Wow! He sounds so sweet!' Roxanne exclaimed with surprise once I'd promised to take her to Joyce Leslie the next day.

'He is sweet! Just because he's a sadist doesn't mean he's not sweet. If there's one thing I've learned from the S&M scene it's that some of the nicest people you'd ever want to meet are practising sadists,' I declared. 'It's the ones without a safe outlet that aren't nice people.'

Roxanne agreed and we made plans to meet for shopping in the late afternoon – provided I was awake and recovered. Then I hung up the phone and took a nap. Two hours later my master called. 'Hey, baby.'

'Hey there!' I greeted him excitedly. 'How are you? Tired?'

'A little. I'm OK. It's been a busy week. I've got to go onstage in a few minutes. We need to figure out what you're going to wear tonight.'

'OK – just keep in mind that I'm going dancing. I have to wear boots for dancing and something comfortable. Is a silver baby doll dress all right?' I tried, having already decided.

'Yes, that's fine. Just make sure you wear old stockings.'

'Old stockings?'

'Yes, so I can rip them off of you,' he growled. 'I feel like a beast tonight.'

'Uh, OK.'

'And cuffs – bring your leather cuffs with you!' David enthused.

'My collar too?'

'What?'

'My leather collar. Should I bring that again?'

'Of course!' David exclaimed like I'd just asked the stupidest question in the world. 'Always!'

'Oh. Anything else?' I asked, searching for a pen and notepad. I was going to have to make a list.

'I want perfume. Perfume *everywhere*.'

'Everywhere?' I repeated, taking notes.

'Yes. I want to smell you when I come.'

'OK.'

'Oh – and no bra.'

'But I have to wear a bra dancing. I'll take it off before I come over,' I promised.

'Good.' David paused. 'I think I'll fuck you in the pussy tonight.'

'You didn't do that last time. How come?'

'I like variety.'

'Well, I have to warn you that I might be a bad girl tonight.'

'And why is that?'

'I get really feisty and aggressive when I dance. I guess from the adrenaline rush.'

'Really? So what does that mean?' he asked curiously.

'It means I might not do everything you tell me to do,' I teased.

'Do you remember last time?'

'Of course. How could I forget?'

'Then you know what happens if you don't obey me. You'll get fucked in the ass,' he countered nonchalantly. I suddenly thought twice about testing this man. 'Mmm,' David growled in my ear. 'I'm completely hard and I'm not even touching myself. I should call you before every show.' I laughed, listening to the sound of dancers milling about in the background. 'I've got to go onstage now, baby. See you tonight.'

'Wait!' I interjected. 'Then I should call you between three and four tonight?'

'Yes, call at tree-thirty.'

'That'll be enough time?'

'Uh-huh. Bye, baby.'

I set down the phone and checked my list twice, wondering how I was ever going to keep my mind on dancing until 'tree'-thirty.

Fortunately, 'La Nueva Escuelita' turned out to be a somewhat amusing if not downright bizarre diversion. Between the Latin go-go boys, drag queens lip-synching in Spanish, and the three-hundred-pound 'hostess' doing Bette Midler doing Janis Joplin in *The Rose*, I kept myself heavily immersed in more camp than I'd seen all year. Add to that the fact that I was the only biological female in a dress and make-up and was getting cruised left and right by mistaken trannie chasers and it made for one interesting evening. By three-thirty I was ready to get the hell out of there.

I called David from a pay phone in the club. 'Are you ready for me?' I shouted into the receiver once he'd answered.

'Yup.'

'Give me about fifteen minutes!'

'OK.'

Jimmy escorted me to David's hotel where I gave him a quick kiss goodbye then wandered into the lobby and over to the elevator located beside a sign reading 'stairs'. Bingo! I climbed one flight up where I was immediately hit with a pungent aroma leading me to Room 204. David answered my knock wearing nothing but bulge-defining briefs. 'You're going to get into trouble,' I teased. 'I can smell the pot smoke all the way down the hall.'

'Really?' he asked then immediately grabbed a glass bottle, spraying the doorway.

'I don't think that's going to help. Your cologne smells nice, though,' I added, removing my coat.

Quickly David grabbed me from behind, rubbing his growing erection against my ass. His strong hands caressed the length of my body then fiddled with my black pantyhose, tearing them at the crotch. He released me from his hold and walked over to the bed, draping himself across it on his stomach. 'So how was your evening?' he asked as he messed around with the portable DVD player on the nightstand.

'Weird. I was at a gay Latin club. The drag queens lip-synched in Spanish.' David just shook his head and laughed. 'How was your night?' I asked.

'Long. I did eight shows and saw eight clients. I had to be hard sixteen times today!'

'Holy shit! And you're not on Viagra?'

'Of course not! I don't need that stuff,' David

answered, offended. 'Do I look like I have a problem?'

'No, I'm just surprised you can still get hard for me after all that,' I explained, flattered to be fucking an X-rated superhero.

'I only have to *get hard* for them. I don't come. After being with guys all day – and then I see you. It's not like I come home to you every night. Of course I get hard – especially with a girl like you.'

I tried not to blush like a schoolgirl. 'So you never come with your clients? Why not?'

'I don't want to,' David stated simply as the DVD stopped on a scene of two guys jerking off in an insatiable blonde's mouth. 'Sometimes I don't even get hard. Actually, I didn't get hard with the last two clients today,' he corrected himself. 'The first guy just wanted to give me a massage for an hour. Two hundred bucks, thank you very much. The second guy wanted to suck my toes. Two hundred bucks, thank you very much.'

'Wow – that's just like at the dungeons! A foot fetish session!' I may as well have been screwing a dominatrix.

Once again David just shook his head and laughed in reflection. 'I went into the bathroom to wash off my feet and when I came back out –'

'The guy was eating your socks!' I interjected.

Nodding vigorously, David laughed even harder. 'Yup – *and* the shoes!'

'Typical,' I concurred as I suddenly remembered I was still wearing my bra but no collar. Discreetly I removed my leather gear from my purse and my sports bra from my chest while David went into the bathroom. 'So how come you're so popular with clients?' I asked, adjusting the black strap around my neck as he returned to the room.

'Because I love what I do. It's my trip.'

'You love making them worship a straight boy? You love torturing them?'

David nodded. 'It's all about the money for me.'

'So basically you're a cocktease.'

David nodded again smugly. Without a word, he approached me and tugged harshly at my nipples through my baby doll dress. Since my period was due any day my breasts were ultra sensitive and I dropped to my knees attempting to endure as much pain as I could. With eyes closed and teeth gritted I finally cried 'mercy'.

David stopped twisting my sore tits. 'Look at me!' he commanded but I continued to keep my eyes shut so he repeated his order again. Slowly I opened my eyes. 'Are you back? Are you with me now?' David barked.

I nodded. 'Yes, sir.'

'Good. Now stand up.' David reached under my dress, through the hole in the crotch, beneath my panties. His fingers opened my pussy, moving fast inside me until I was soaked. 'You're wet like a slut,' David whispered accusingly, his breath hot on my cheek.

'You make me wet, sir.'

He stuck a damp index finger between my teeth so I obediently began to suck seductively. 'Give me your tongue.' I opened my mouth to my master and he inhaled my tongue like a vacuum. Instinctively, I pulled away. 'I said to give me your tongue!' David ordered menacingly. I did – then moved back once more. 'OK. You don't want to do as you're told? Bend over!'

Sitting down, David threw me over his leg and smacked my ass hard. 'Sorry, sir,' I whispered.

'What?' David barked, hitting me again.

'Sorry, sir!' I cried out.

He brought me up onto my feet. 'Go get the lube. It's on the bed. Bring it over here and then get down on your knees.'

I stared at the mattress, desperately trying to figure out what the hell he was asking for. Then I saw the bottle of Wet in the middle of the queen-sized bed. I walked to where my master sat calmly on the chair by the little wooden table then presented it to him on my knees. Setting the lubricant aside, he dangled two tiny clamps connected by a metal chain in front of my face. Nipple clamps. PMS. Great.

'It's right before my period. I don't think I can take those, sir.'

Nodding, David placed the alligator clips on the nightstand then removed his briefs to reveal a porn-sized hard-on. 'Lick my balls,' he said tonelessly and lit a cigarette. I sampled the shaved scrotum with my tongue, sucking one heavy testicle then the other into my mouth, before moving on to his pleading cock. 'I said *my balls – not my dick!*' David barked. Startled, I tried to obey orders but my master yanked me up by my hair. 'Take off your dress. On the bed.'

Impatiently, David slipped the condom on himself then joined me bearing the bottle of Wet, soaking two fingers before shoving them in and out of my pussy with zeal. Murmurs of pleasure emanated from the DVD as David tore the destroyed pantyhose and drenched undies from my body. Carelessly he tossed them to the floor then rolled onto his back beside me. 'Get on top of me. On your back.'

Without any warning David was inside me thrusting hard. As I raised my torso to match his movements he immediately yanked me back by the hair. I

attempted the more comfortable position again –
and felt a hand wrap tightly around my throat.
Testing him, I tried to break away one last time.
'Where do you think you're going?' he snapped,
affirming that I'd lost all control.

With pleasure I turned my body over to my master
as he pushed me up to a sitting position then onto my
knees, using me like a dog. As cries of ecstasy came
from the DVD I contemplated synchronising my own
moans to those of the technological orgy. 'Oh, shit!
I'm gonna come,' David declared so he took a deep
breath and pulled out. A finger forced cold lube up
my ass, soon to be replaced by what was unmistak-
ably David's long hard cock.

'Ow! Ow! Ow! Ow!' I yelled as he penetrated me.

'Sorry! Sorry!' David yelled back and extricated
himself from my tight asshole. 'I got too excited.'

'You got too excited? That's good. You know, you
don't have to fuck my ass if you don't want to,' I
suggested.

David returned his dick to my pussy, grunting and
drilling the wet hole with an intensity that made the
DVD porn stars sound like amateurs. For his grand
finale he climaxed with a cry loud enough to summon
hotel security. Exhausted, I lay still on the bed, his
orgasm still shaking my body as he went into the
bathroom. The toilet flushed and he peeked out to flash
his rogue's smile at me before turning on the shower.
This was better than any XXX film I'd ever seen!

Emerging fresh and clean, David walked to the
wooden table. 'Chocolate?' he offered, taking a piece
of candy from a Godiva box.

'No, thanks,' I answered, declining his client's gift.
David popped one in his mouth with a shrug. 'I want
a massage.'

'Ah, yes! A massage! I'd love one!' he exclaimed, rubbing his hands together excitedly.

'No, no, no. *I* want a massage,' I repeated.

'Oh? *You* want a massage?' David mocked.

'Yeah! I'm in control now!' I declared, ready for battle now that the war was safely over.

'In control of what?' David asked, biting into another pricey piece of chocolate.

'Uh – my massage,' I answered lamely.

'Uh-huh. OK, I'll give you a massage,' David relented. He caressed my back as I lay on my stomach, reaching to shut off the DVD before letting his hands wander down to my butt. 'Have you ever bottomed before?' I asked as his fingers drifted to the back of my thigh.

'Nope.'

'Never? Not even for a girl?' I probed curiously.

'No. I'm a top.'

'So you'd never bottom ever?'

'No.'

'So do I suck cock like a guy or a girl?' I continued lazily as his fingers slowly began their own probe.

'A girl.'

'Really?' I was shocked – and quite offended. 'But guys suck better!'

'Not true. Not all guys. You suck like a girl. You suck good, though,' he reassured me.

'What does a guy suck like?'

'Usually guys try to take it down their throat – which is not always good. It hurts.'

'It hurts you?'

'Sure! My cock slamming against the back of a throat?'

'I guess.' From the receiving end I wouldn't know. David's pussy-play was making me wet all over again.

'Hey! You're supposed to be massaging me – not making me horny!'

'I want to come in your mouth.'

I craned my neck to catch a glimpse of his rock-hard cock. 'You want to come again? You just came!' David nodded. 'OK,' I agreed, surprised by his virility.

After flipping me onto my back he positioned himself above my head. 'Open your mouth.' I yawned as wide as I could while David jerked his massive dick until warm cum started to dribble between my waiting lips. 'That is the sexiest thing in the world!' David declared.

Holding the full load in my mouth I motioned for one of the tissues he was using. He smiled as I spit. 'You want a massage now?' I offered once I could talk. David nodded vigorously. 'OK. Lie down,' I commanded and happily he obeyed. I fondled his perfect bodybuilder's physique all the way from the top of his broad shoulders to the bottom of his muscular calves. By the time I'd gotten to his unbelievably firm buttocks I was feeling sleepy. I finished rubbing his legs then rolled over beside him. 'I'm tired. Can I crash here?'

'Sure. I have a client tomorrow, though.'

'What time?'

'Eleven. He wants to take me out to breakfast first.'

'You have to go to breakfast with him?'

'No! No way! He just wants to,' David explained as he stuck *Se7en* into the DVD. I could hear Brad Pitt speaking English.

'You don't have it in French?'

'No, I do. You can't watch it in French, though.'

'Well, what other movies do you have? Besides porno.'

'*Predator*.'

'Schwarzenegger?'

'Yeah.'

'Action-adventure movies put you to sleep, too?' David nodded. 'What keeps you awake – boring love stories?' I chuckled. 'No, that's OK. I can try to watch *Se7en* in French. I'll get used to it.' David fiddled with the player until Brad Pitt was speaking like the Parisian he isn't. 'Whoa! How many languages can you watch it in?'

'A lot. I don't know.'

'Can you watch it in, like, Portuguese?' It was time for me to retire my VCR.

'Probably.'

'Let's watch it in Portuguese then!' I exclaimed, rising excitedly.

'No! I don't speak Portuguese.'

'So what? Neither do I!'

David ignored me so I lay back down and, surprisingly, found myself actually drifting off to the sound of what I imagined to be Brad Pitt emoting for Godard. I was nearly asleep when I felt David get up. Through half-open eyes I saw him return with his box of chocolates and crawl into bed beside me. As my lids fluttered shut his hand lightly patted the top of my head.

'Goodnight,' he sing-songed. Opening my eyes I smiled back at the caring face that beamed above me. Then I fell deep into another dream.

I was out like a light until I heard David shout something in French and then 'Baby, baby, you've got to get up.' Startled, I immediately sat up. That's when I noticed there was French coming from the other side of the door as well – and it sure as hell wasn't Brad Pitt! 'Twenty minutes!' David yelled back at the male voice.

The unseen man said something else in French so David shouted again in his native tongue. I hadn't a clue as to what was going on until they switched to English and I realised it was his client on the other side. I hurried to dress.

'Just give me twenty minutes, OK?' David called, then to me, 'Baby, baby, don't rush. It's Sunday. Take your time. He'll wait.'

'What? You're just going to let him stand out there for twenty minutes?' I whispered.

David shrugged nonchalantly. 'Yeah.'

Yes, I really was screwing a dominatrix. The client tried again in French.

'What? What do you have for me?' David asked, clearly annoyed.

'Uh, coffee,' he answered meekly.

Without even bothering to get out of bed David reached over and pulled open the door just wide enough so the forty-something businessman could see me trying to gather my things. The guy handed David a paper bag and quickly glanced my way. He couldn't get out of there fast enough. After shutting the door David rose to light a cigarette.

'Why does he speak French?' I asked.

'He learned it somewhere,' David sighed, taking a cup of coffee and bagel from the bag. The phone rang as he unwrapped breakfast. 'Hello?' David switched to French as I searched the room for my pantyhose. I finally found them in a corner, looking like they'd been through a shredder. All evidence destroyed.

After hanging up David came over to where I was trying to salvage my hose in order to make it home without being harassed. Bare legs and a mini-dress in below-freezing weather just didn't cut it on the subway. 'The guy's apologising to me over and over

– saying he can reschedule,' David explained. 'I don't think so! Bitch woke me up!'

He sipped his coffee as I displayed my pantyhose's remains. 'I think they're dead. I'm going to get hassled on the subway for my bare legs.'

'You want to get another pair before you go home? You need money?' he asked, opening the drawer of the little wooden table.

'No, I'm OK. I'll just take a cab.' David held me close, his pelvis thrusting against my crotch. 'What are you doing?'

'Thinking about sex.'

'Well, your client will take care of that.'

'It's not the same.'

'So will I see you again before you leave?' I asked hopefully.

'I don't think so, baby. Tonight I'm going to get really fucked up.'

'Why?'

'It's just the mood I'm in right now. It's been a very long week.'

'OK. So when are you coming back?' I tried.

'Don't know until tonight,' David answered and took a bite of bagel.

'Well, I guess I'll see you whenever that is.'

David nodded and kissed me. He tasted like cinnamon. 'Have a good day, baby,' he said as he escorted me to the door.

'Have a good trip.'

I descended the stairs, walked through the lobby, and emerged into the Sunday morning sun feeling unsure of everything – everything, that is, except for being in love with the way David made me feel.

The Claiming

(April 2000)

David had arrived in New York on Monday. I knew
because I'd forced Derek, my own personal fag hag,
to call the Gaiety to ask when David would be
dancing again (since the owner Denise was wary
about giving information to women, probably figuring jealous ex-girlfriends stalking straight strippers in
a gay club was one more headache she didn't need).

So when Thursday morning came with no call from
my master, I convinced Jimmy to forego his gym time
Friday in favour of stalking David at the early evening
show. By late that afternoon I felt less stressed knowing
that I would still see David – even if he didn't want to
see me. Arriving home from work I heard my
answering machine pick up so I rushed inside, my heart
filling with hope, and leapt across my living room –
only to reach my sister's voice droning on about some
apartment she wanted us to look at the next day.
Disappointed, I let her talk her way to the end of the
beep before hitting 'play' to retrieve my other messages.

'Hey, Lauren. It's your friend David. Just wanted
to let you know I'm in town for the week. It's been
pretty busy here. Call me if you want to and let me

know what you are doing tonight. 221-2600, the room is 205. That's 221-2600 – the room is 205. Call me, let me know either way or maybe we can see each other later in the week.'

My entire body was pounding with joy. His voice was self-assured, but slightly nervous, the tone of a man who feared he might be setting himself up for disappointment. For the first time since we'd met back in December I realised I wasn't on a one-way street – he was as worried I might not want to see him as I was afraid he wouldn't phone! I dialled the hotel and left a message. An hour later he called.

'Hey, baby, what are you doing tonight?' David asked, already knowing the answer.

'Nothing,' I said coyly.

'Wanna be my sex toy?'

'I always want to be your sex toy.'

'Good, good,' he sighed. The connection was so strong I thought I could hear his hard-on through the line. 'Do you have a whip?'

'What?'

'A whip. I would like to play with a whip tonight.'

'I think I might.' I had a whip I used as a stage prop during my lip-synching with the drag queens of Pyramid Club days. 'I'll have to look around for it.'

'Good. Bring that. And wear high heels – and socks –'

'Stockings.'

'Yes. And wear –'

'I already know what I'm going to wear,' I interrupted boldly, thinking of the lavender latex dress I'd found at a vintage clothing store in Williamsburg for twenty bucks. 'I know what you like.'

'Good. I like surprises,' David said pleased. 'Oh – and can you get me something to smoke? I pay you when you get here.'

'Hmmm. I'll try. I'll have to call my friend Roxanne. She's the only person I know who smokes pot.'

'OK. You're going to be sweet for me tonight, right?'

'Of course!' I declared.

'You will be nice and sweet and submissive,' David continued, lingering on each word so I could absorb his orders.

'Mmm-hmm.'

'So I call you at home? You're not going out tonight?'

'No. I'm working.'

'On what?'

'On the script for my debut feature film,' I proudly announced.

'Ahh!' David exclaimed. 'What's it about?'

I disclosed the storyline for each part of my psychosexual trilogy, grandly pausing before I revealed that the last involved a gay-for-pay stripper. David laughed heartily. 'Can I use your words as dialogue?' I asked.

'Sure, of course. You can use whatever you want,' he agreed, flattered.

I made a mental note to get that in writing. 'So, do you have any clients tonight?'

'Probably. I don't know,' he hedged. 'But I'll save all my energy for you.'

'Good,' I said, flattered too. When I got off the phone I decided I might as well take a crack at the script. Not that spending the evening typing David's and my words into the dialogue between Joe and Lois was going to make the minutes between me and my master tick by any faster, but at least I'd lengthen my screenplay's running time.

I finished with the scene and was all ready to go in sleek lavender latex, black nylons and high heels when David called at half past midnight. 'Hey, baby. I'm running a little late. I should be ready for you at one.'

I hadn't been able to score any pot from Roxanne and I couldn't locate my whip. But I didn't tell David that, not wanting to let him dwell too long on my punishment. He'd find out soon enough what a bad girl I'd been. 'You want to call me at one or you want me to be there at one?'

'No. I want you to *be here* at one,' David snapped, displeased with having to repeat his instructions.

'OK. I'll be there at one,' I assured him.

I grabbed my coat and tossed into my purse a pair of cheesy furry leopard-print handcuffs that Roxanne had given me as a joke birthday gift the year before. It was the only sex toy I owned besides my leather restraints, which lacked any fastening device for the rings. Oh, boy, I was going to pay for this dearly, I half-worried and hoped. The only thing I did manage to do correctly was arrive at David's hotel at one on the dot. Maybe my punctuality would score some slave points. I hurried through the exact same lobby I'd walked through two months earlier and past the clerk with the suspicious eyes. This time, though, I knew exactly where the stairs were and ascended confidently to the second floor.

I knocked softly on the door to Room 205. Within seconds David answered, a wicked smile forming on his face as I took off my coat. Wordlessly he went to the phone to continue listening to his messages while he chomped away on McDonald's fries. I set my purse and jacket on top of his suitcase then lay back on the bed to focus on the hotel porn playing, two guys on one girl. I smiled to myself.

David put down the receiver and gazed my way. 'The guy I just saw couldn't get it up – too coked out. How are you, baby?'

'Good, except I fucked up,' I said, laughing self-consciously.

'What do you mean?'

'Well, I thought I had a whip but I don't anymore. And I couldn't get Roxanne to get you any pot. Oh – and I forgot to shave,' I added, figuring if I was going to confess I might as well run down my entire list of sins.

David looked at me and slowly shook his head in disappointment. 'You fuck up, you need to be punished.'

'I brought these, though,' I offered hopefully, taking my handcuffs from my purse. David responded with a hard stare that said I was crazy if I thought a pair of fur handcuffs was going to cut it. 'Sorry.' He returned to his French fries and porno. 'I like that,' I finally announced, breaking the sound of orgasmic moans.

'Like what?'

'That – two guys and one girl.'

'Why didn't you tell me this before? I could have gotten a friend,' David said nonchalantly.

For a second I was startled speechless. 'You didn't ask.'

'Well, I have a lot of friends. We could do that if you want.'

'I'd love to do that!' I enthused.

David rocked back on the legs of his chair as he addressed the porn stars on the screen. 'She can't find her whip, she doesn't bring me pot, she hasn't shaved – and she wants me to get her another guy! Uh-huh!' he added sarcastically. I started to giggle. 'Have you done it before?' he wondered, meeting my eye.

'No.'

'Well, if I get you a friend you have to get me one.'

'But I don't know any girls I could bring!' I protested. 'I only know gay guys!'

'Guy, girl, whatever,' David sighed, stunning me silent once again. Wow – this guy sure knew his way into my kinky heart! I flipped onto my stomach and David ran his hand up the back of my thigh and over my butt as he finished his greasy potatoes. 'Take off your stockings and get down on your knees in front of me.'

'Don't you want to rip them off?' I urged. I'd purposely worn old ones to please him.

'Did I ask you a question?'

'No.'

'Then why are you talking?'

'Sorry, sir.'

I leapt off the bed, quickly removed my nylons then knelt in obedience. I gazed upwards, drinking in his body with my eyes for the first time in two months. He was wearing his usual jeans and sneakers and a black netted top that covered not one inch of his powerful tan chest and biceps. When he looked down I instinctively turned my attention to the floor.

'Take off my shoes. I need a foot massage. Unsnap the buckles first.' I stripped both big feet bare, working my fingers into the tired soles as David groaned his praise. Lighting a cigarette, he leaned back in his chair. 'So, do you have any interesting stories for me? Any new experiences?'

I thought of Antonio, the sexy muscular 'totally Lauren's type' Latin bouncer Aimee had discovered at her new job managing a dance club. Unfortunately, the club was in Iceland. I hesitated before blurting out, 'Uh, phone sex.'

'You had phone sex? With a guy?'

'Mmm-hmm.'

David was intrigued, putting me on the spot. 'And what did you do?'

I blushed with embarrassment, though I wasn't sure if it stemmed from being forced to expose the details of my naughty behaviour or having to hide that Antonio was, as fate would have it, also a stripper who knew David from the Gaiety. 'He told me to put my finger inside myself and to imagine it was his tongue.'

'Mmm-hmm. And what else?' David inquired, lifting his left foot to me.

'Um, I asked him what his cock looked like.'

'Big or small?'

'Big.'

'And you like that?'

'Yes – especially when it's hard,' I answered softly.

'OK,' David stated, planting both feet firmly on the floor, 'now take off my pants.' After he helped me undo his jeans I unleashed his enormous erection. 'Put that big cock in your mouth,' he commanded tonelessly. I opened my bronze-coloured lips in submission. 'Mmm,' David moaned, slamming the tip of his dick against the back of my throat. 'You're going to be sore for two days. I'm going to fuck you everywhere. In every hole,' he threatened, grabbing hold of my hair and wrenching me from his hard-on. 'Get up. On all fours on the other side of the bed.'

As I scrambled to obey, David went into the bathroom. The familiar hum of his electric razor alerted me to what was next on the S&M agenda. Reappearing from behind, David stripped off my panties, hoisted up my purple latex dress then ran the instrument along my delicate skin. 'Look at this! I can't even trust you to shave yourself!' he exclaimed in disgust, slapping my right buttock hard. I tried to focus on the buzzing noise, the sound of shame, until David was done grooming my pussy and ass. Deftly he dragged me to my feet by the collar I'd actually remembered to wear, and all the way up to the tips of my toes, forcing my face directly into his own.

'I don't think you know who's in control here,' he observed. 'You'd better learn. Into the bathroom.' He released my collar menacingly and I zoomed into the bathroom, my master on my high heels. He turned on the faucet and motioned for me to sit on the toilet. Then he ran his fingers under the water for what seemed an eternity. As I waited, I noticed a peculiar odour. It took me a minute to realise he'd lit a joint at some point during our play. Now the smell was making me sick. 'Shit – no hot water!' David finally declared, offering me a lukewarm washcloth. 'This is it. Clean yourself off.'

Gently I wiped my hairless pussy and between my butt cheeks. 'Can you open a window, sir?' I asked meekly, handing him the used towel.

'Why?' David wondered as he took it.

Unfortunately, I thought he had said 'way', which is what he used for 'yeah', which thankfully my trilingual friend Aimee had explained was French slang for *oui*. But he didn't move so, confused, I repeated my request. 'A window. Can you open one, sir?'

'Why?' David asked once again, becoming concerned.

'Pot smoke.'

'Oh, sorry!' he exclaimed, remembering I wasn't a stoner. Then he rushed out of the bathroom to let in some fresh air. Moments later David returned to pry my thighs wide open and study his work. His left hand shot to my throat, applying pressure to the collar as the fingers of his right slow-danced deep inside my pussy. I closed my eyes and absorbed the cool breeze blowing in until David released his grip. Silently I watched him pick up a can of shaving cream, spraying the contents into his palm before massaging it into my crotch. Then with my pussy engulfed in white foam David lit a cigarette and, with utmost care, took a wet razor to my freshly clipped skin. So focused was he on not cutting me he didn't even notice when the tip of his Dunhill touched my inner thigh. Instead of crying out in pain, though, I began to laugh at the absurdity.

'Ow! Ow! You're burning me with your cigarette!' I said between giggles.

David immediately disposed of his Dunhill in the sink, but not before my laughter became contagious. Once we'd both regained our composure David finished his delicate shaving job then wiped my crotch clean. 'Look at this. I'm hard as a rock,' he sighed, pointing to his huge erection. He popped the cap from a solid deodorant stick and rubbed it over my pussy.

'What's that for?' I asked.

'So it doesn't get red. It's good for your skin.' He pulled me up off the toilet. 'Get on the bed. I'm going to fuck you doggy style.'

I climbed onto the mattress, shoving the furry handcuffs and matching keys to the side as David followed, hoisting my dress to my waist. I heard a condom tear and moments later felt his thick dick inside my pussy, pounding hard. My entire attention focused on not flying face-first into the headboard and it took me a minute to notice the lubricated fingers fondling my butt. But by then David had pulled out and his warm tongue was inside my asshole then my pussy, his mouth pushing so hard that I finally hit the headboard. Roughly he dragged me back so he could ram my pussy once again. Reaching for the cheesy restraints while simultaneously pinning my hands behind my back, he wrapped the fur-lined metal around my wrists.

David was fucking me so hard I had the image of a jackhammer drilling my wet hole. It was almost as if his cock weren't enough – he wanted to put his entire being inside me. Desperately I tried to take it all, but the furry bastards were cutting into my skin. 'Mercy! Mercy!' I yelled and David froze. 'The cuffs – they hurt.' Gently he tried to remove them while keeping his dick firmly inside. 'You need the key,' I suggested.

'No, I don't,' he said, sliding them from my wrists. Then he resumed drilling my pussy without missing a beat. 'Give me your hand.' I turned up my right palm behind my back and David squirted lube onto my fingers. 'Put your finger in your ass.' Slowly I obeyed orders as David thrust to his own rhythm. 'Put my dick inside,' he finally whispered in my ear, tugging my finger from the hole. I reached around for his slick erection and David helped me help him inside. 'Push down,' he groaned.

It was like a wild animal had been released. A jackhammer actually would have been more bearable. The only thing that stopped me from crying mercy were the sweet and tender kisses David was showering all over my back and neck. Unfortunately, my tight asshole didn't care what the hell was going on with any of my other body parts. 'Mercy!' I shouted when finally I could take no more. David flipped me over, single-handedly securing my legs above my head. Then he forced his fat cock back inside – my ass. 'Ow! It hurts!' I whimpered through clenched teeth.

David held still to meet my eyes with a look that lied *this is hurting me more than it is you*. 'You need to be punished,' he quietly explained. 'You need to learn who has the control.' Then he resumed his rough ass fuck. With teeth gritted I was on the verge of stopping him yet again. 'Look at you! You can't even take this?' David taunted then turned his attention to the porn stars on the TV. 'And she thinks she can take two guys?'

In a flash my pride told my sore hole to fuck off. 'Yes, I can, sir!' I exclaimed through my clenched teeth.

'No, I don't think you can,' David dared, pushing deeper.

'Yes, I can, sir!' I repeated defiantly.

'Show me,' David challenged me. 'Stick a finger inside.' I slid my index finger into my pussy and was shocked to feel David's enormous cock through my own skin. The sensation was quite eerie, like I was touching him inside someone else's body. 'Good,' David sighed. 'Can you stick two fingers in?' My teeth were grinding as my middle finger joined the index. 'OK. Now three.'

I easily could have done three but by now the pain in my ass had vanquished all pride. It was all I could do just to keep from crying mercy.

'Only two fingers? That's not a very big dick!' David mocked, moving fast inside my ass.

'Mercy!' I screamed.

David shot me a look to kill, eyes filled with disgust. I felt like the worst little girl in the world. He hung his head, shaking it sadly. 'Every time I get going you stop me. OK – that's it!' He pulled out and hopped from the mattress. 'Off! Off the bed! On your knees!'

As I knelt to the floor David came behind me, harshly shoving me onto all fours. After taking a seat on a chair, he dragged me backwards then punished my pussy with his dissatisfied dick. The pain was nearly as bad as anal penetration. A jackhammer pounding furiously inside me still felt like a jackhammer regardless of which orifice David used. I tried to absorb my master's thrusts with my own moans.

Fortunately, David soon stopped his drilling and walked around to stand before me. Grabbing my head by the nape he tilted it upwards, removed his condom and began to jerk off. 'Open that mouth! Wide!' David ordered as drops of fresh semen sprinkled my lips. Then came the volcanic eruption, ejaculate overflowing onto my surprised face and all down the front of my new latex dress. His erection emptied, he collapsed onto the bed with a loud groan.

I climbed up and sneaked on top of him. He smiled. 'Give me a minute to clean up. Then you can give me a massage.' He went into the bathroom, returning with a lukewarm washcloth for me. I wiped my face and cum-soaked dress.

'I hope latex doesn't stain,' I said.

'Want me to jack off all over it to make it even?'

'Yeah. I'll leave it for your clients.' David laughed as he went back to the bathroom to rinse his own body clean. 'If every guy was like you I'd be fucking all the time!' I called out in confession. 'Most guys suck. You know how girls always say if they sleep with a guy on the first date then the guy won't call them back? Well, I have the opposite problem! I sleep with them once and they think I'm their fucking girlfriend. That we're in some sort of monogamous relationship! Suddenly they want to take me out to dinner. If I wanted to do dinner, we would have already done it! Where are all these guys who just want to fuck?'

David emerged still laughing and lay on the bed beside me. 'Everyone wants to fuck. See, if I'm going to have sex I want it to be good. I don't need some sort of receptacle for my semen. I'd just as soon jerk off to my porno.'

'Exactly!' I agreed.

'I'm actually too much for most girls.'

I could believe that. He was a virtual one-man-gang-bang. 'Well, I'm too much for most guys!'

'I picked this girl up at a party a couple weeks ago,' David continued. 'I was tripping on ecstasy and I wanted to fuck so I took her home and she was so boring I had to tell her to leave.'

'You kicked her out during sex?' I thought only Roxanne did those things.

'Sure. She was boring. I told her to leave so I could jack off to my porno.'

I went into a giggle fit. David stretched out on his stomach and I straddled his torso to give him a massage. Rolling my palms along the muscles of his perfect body was like kneading steel. My hands caressed his solid calves up to his strong thighs and over the cold hard buttocks that I could have bounced a quarter off of. David groaned approvingly. I fondled his wide back and the action star biceps that could make all the Chelsea queens drool. 'I love your arms,' I whispered into David's ear. 'I wish I had arms like these.' David just laughed. How relaxing it was not to have to censor myself, I thought. How

71

wonderful to be with someone who wasn't going to look at me like I was a freak – or if he did it was with a sense of camaraderie!

When I was finished David rose to replace the porno with a French-Canadian western. 'No *Se7en*?' I asked surprised.

'It's on DVD.'

Of course. Silly me. David brought out his DVD player and I crawled beside him to watch. As I gazed at the tiny screen displaying the multilingual Brad Pitt, David suddenly leaned over to impulsively place a tender kiss on the top of my head. I was stunned. I gave his left thigh a squeeze and we sat there awkwardly for a moment. Then he turned to look at me. 'I like you,' he said with a smile.

'Well, I like you, too,' I laughed self-consciously. 'I wish you were around more often.'

'So what type of guy do you want?' David inquired, changing the subject.

'Mmm. Latin. Do you have any Spanish guys?' Was there some sort of catalogue I should be browsing?

'No, I don't think we have any this week.'

Darn, all out of my colour. 'Well, dark then – like you. A brunette. No blonds. I hate blonds. And none of those all-American types – yuck!' I added, straightening my stockings.

'What type? Gay or straight?'

'No gay boys!' I ordered, securing my heels. 'I hate gay boys. No queens. I want a manly guy.'

David nodded as I bundled into my coat. 'I'll look around for you.'

'Tell you what – I'll score you some pot if you score me a guy. Deal?'

David nodded again and we kissed. Then I sauntered out the door, my spirit soaring. Recently

Roxanne had disclosed that she didn't want a boy-friend so much as a partner-in-crime. I couldn't wait to tell her that I'd finally found mine.

On Sunday morning I awoke to a flurry of white outside my window. Wasn't I wearing shorts and a tank top just the day before? It was the ninth of April and New York City had gone from seventy degrees to thirty in less than twenty-four hours. I guess I should have realised that a freak snowstorm was simply an omen of things to come.

The clock read noon as I lazily dressed. The phone rang. 'Hello?' I yawned into the receiver.

'Hey,' said the male voice on the other side.

'Hey,' I replied nonchalantly, guessing it was my phone sex stripper. He sounded tired. 'Did you just get up?'

'Yup, I didn't finish work until five in the morning.' As the French accent emerged my heart raced with joy. 'What are you doing?'

'Um, right now I'm getting dressed. I have to go look at an apartment with my sister later in the afternoon.'

'You're moving?'

'Trying to. I want to move out to Brooklyn. What are you doing? You have a show, right?'

'Yes, but no clients yet. My show's not until tree-thirty. I have to do some things. I want to get some breakfast and then go over to Sony for some computer stuff. Want to come over?'

'Sure,' I answered excitedly, 'but I still need to get dressed.'

'How long will that take?'

'About a half hour, I guess. Why don't you go get breakfast and call me when you're done eating?' I suggested. 'I should be ready by then.'

'OK, baby.'

'Talk to you later.' I hung up then made a mad dash to get my make-up on and to put my body into some form of oxymoronic sexy winter wear. I was slipping into a pair of tight black bellbottom pants when the phone rang. I rushed to the receiver.

'Hey, there!' Jimmy greeted me effervescently. 'You're not gonna believe what I got last night! Hot Latin cock! Nah, nah, nah, nah, nah – I got it before you did! And he was fun! Argentinian, too!'

'Uh-huh. I'm trying to get ready to go meet my master, Jimmy.'

'Oops – sorry! I'll call you later!'

Jimmy promptly disconnected. I tried to set the receiver in its cradle but it rang again in my hand. 'Hello?'

'Hey, Lauren!' chimed Derek from the other end.

'Hey, there. I hope you didn't have a one-night stand last night because I'm on my way out to meet David.'

'Oops – talk to you later! Bye!'

After hearing a dial tone I managed to actually put the receiver down before it sounded again. 'Hello?' I answered, becoming exasperated.

'Hey, baby!' exclaimed the French-accented voice. Whew!

'Are you done eating?'

'Mmm-hmm. Are you ready?'

'Yup, I'll be out the door in two minutes.'

'OK. I'll meet you down in the lobby then.'

I gathered my coat and purse and trekked out into the April snow. Not in the mood to deal with the slow weekend Eighth Avenue subway, I hailed a cab and headed uptown. The taxi dropped me at 46th Street and I walked through heavy flurries into the hotel lobby where I spied David chatting with the hotel clerk, his back towards me. As I entered the concierge looked up and David whirled around. 'Hey – there you are!' he exclaimed, beaming.

'I can't believe it's snowing!' I cried in disbelief.

'I know,' David shrugged – not exactly news to a Québecois. 'Let's catch a cab. I need to run over to the Sony building.' We went outside and hailed a taxi. David opened the door for me, looking incredibly manly in his jeans and baseball cap. 'Can you take us to the Sony building? It's up on Madison, I think,' he told the driver.

Luckily, the cabby knew how to get there. Like a true Villager I saw no need to shop above 14th Street so I couldn't be of any help. 'What do you need there?' I asked.

'I'm trying to get my computer set up. They're all sold out of what I need in Canada,' David explained, placing his palm on my inner thigh. 'I like these,' he praised, running his hand along the black cotton fabric.

'Good.' His hand caressed its way up to my crotch. 'You'll have to be careful if you want to play with me,' I warned. 'I got my period.'

'Your ass doesn't have your period,' he nonchalantly noted.

I chuckled at his deadpan tone. 'Sorry if I was a little late getting to the hotel. I couldn't get off the phone. Jimmy wanted to tell me about his one-night stand.'

David laughed, wickedly amused. 'How was it?'

'Good. He told me, "Nah, nah, nah, nah, nah – I got Latin cock before you did!" An Argentinian, I think.'

He laughed even harder. 'You know, you're the only American I will sleep with,' David disclosed. 'Americans are the worst in bed. Why is that?'

'I don't know,' I giggled in wholehearted agreement. 'But it's not just the girls. It's the guys, too. Guess how long it's been since I've slept with an American.'

'How long?'

'Four years!' I declared, holding up four fingers for emphasis.

'Really?' David said, surprised.

'Yeah. I won't do it anymore.'

'One of my friends and I went to a strip club and he was trying to pick up an American girl,' David recalled. 'I told him not to bother. He should just go home and jack off to porno instead. He said, "How do you know she'll be that bad?" I said, "Don't believe me? Just go ahead – you'll see what I mean!"'

I laughed, overcome with a strong sense of solidarity. 'Well, my goal is to fuck one guy from every country before I die,' I revealed honestly. Now David really laughed – but with the utmost approval. It felt good to have common interests.

When the cab stopped at the Sony building I stepped out into the springtime winter wonderland while David paid the driver. Behind the glass doors the computer store was packed with customers and short on staff. Finally, David found a single salesman helping an Asian couple. 'Excuse me, sir,' he interrupted politely before continuing with just the slightest hint of sarcasm. 'Are you the only one who works here?'

'No, but how can I help you?' the guy answered courteously as the Asian tourists talked together in their native tongue.

'Do you have this?' David asked, pointing to a picture of a computer monitor in a Sony booklet he'd brought along.

'Uh, no, we're all sold out.'

David groaned in exasperation. 'OK. Thank you, sir.'

The clerk was kind enough to give David a number to call to place an order and we headed back outside, having wasted a good twenty minutes. David whistled for a cab but none stopped so I flagged one down instead. It paid to be a New Yorker. 'Where are we going?' I asked the master in charge.

'I want to see sex shops, leather stores – show me something exciting!' David announced grandly.

'Christopher and Seventh, I guess,' I told the cabby.

As we rode downtown I asked David to fill me in on all the new experiences he'd had since we'd last seen each other. He thought hard for a moment before responding. 'Hmm, I really can't think of any. I did have two slaves.'

'Male or female?' I interrogated.

'Two guys. I had to dominate them both. When one of the guys set up the appointment I told him, "You'd better be on time, bitch." He goes, "Oh, yes, sir!"' David laughed heartily.

I giggled with delight. 'You know, if you were born into a female body you'd be working as a dominatrix right now.'

'Of course!' David exclaimed as if he'd already thought of it. 'I'd make a fortune!'

'So what happened to our threesome?' I wanted to know.

'There are only two brunettes working this time and they're both here with their girlfriends.'

'So? You like girls!'

'So what?'

'So – an orgy.'

'No!' David countered. 'They won't do it. They're not like me and you – they're boring! I work with the most boring people you could ever imagine,' he sighed. 'All they talk about is money and work. It's scary.'

'I believe that – same thing happens in the S&M business. These people have no lives. Even S&M can get boring if you do it 24/7.'

'Yup,' David agreed. 'It's really frightening,' he added seriously, shaking his head sadly. 'So, did you go out last night?'

'Nope.'

'Being a good girl?'

'That and Lent.'

'What?'

'The nightclub we go to on the weekends is Polish. Polish Catholics are really religious. There are, like, five people in the club during Lent.'

'That's crazy,' David commented, quite amused.

'I know – but it's true. We have to wait until Easter to go dancing.'

'I wanted to call you last night but it was after five and I didn't want to wake you.'

'Yup, I was definitely sleeping.'

'I needed a blow job. It would have been nice to wake up this morning, get a good blow job, go get something to eat –'

'I'd love to give you a blow job,' I mouthed to David, aware the driver was eavesdropping.

'Mmm,' David growled. 'I'm getting hard now.'

'Good – you'll be all ready for your show this afternoon.'

Arriving at our destination, David paid the nosey cabby then cried 'Starbucks!' as he noticed the house of mud on the corner. 'I need coffee. Want something?'

'Blech! I hate Starbucks.' I was a Porto Rico Importing Co. connoisseur through and through. Inside the shop David ordered a cup of java that was taking nearly ten minutes to prepare. 'What the hell did you order?' I wondered.

'Just coffee. Americans – so slow!'

'Watch it – you're talking to one!' I exclaimed mock-offended, faking a left roundhouse kick to his knee. 'And I'm dangerous. I kickbox – so don't mess with me.'

'Don't mess with you?' David harrumphed. 'I used to teach judo and karate when I was in the army. I'll show you who's in control,' he added.

'You were in the Canadian army?' I asked, surprised.

'Uh-huh, Green Berets for four years.'

'So you jumped out of planes with parachutes and shit?'

'Sure.'

'Why?' I shuddered at the thought of free falling hundreds of feet.

'Because I wanted to. I did a lot of things before stripping. I was in the army, I managed bars –' David disclosed before interrupting himself to pay for his long-awaited coffee. I followed him back out into the springtime snow.

'This way,' I said, guiding David up Seventh to The Pleasure Chest.

'Is that an aquarium?' he asked, amazed by the window display.

'Yeah, but it's fake. The window changes with the seasons.'

Once inside the sex shop David and I quickly determined most of the merchandise to be priced for the kinky rich. 'I love toys,' David sighed, admiring a Plexiglas dildo.

'Ouch! That would hurt!'

'It's sculpture. It's not to use,' David explained, handing me the transparent phallus.

'So what's your favourite toy?' I inquired, setting the dildo back in its display.

'Butt plug,' he stated without hesitation. 'You should see all the toys I have at home. I have a whole suitcase full.'

'Don't tell me that! You're making me horny. Oh, look – they have a black one now!' I cried, pointing to 'Tyson', a bald black version of 'Billy' (the gay world's answer to 'Barbie'), propped next to the Latin 'Carlos'. I guess it was only a matter of time.

'What is that?' David asked.

'It's Tyson,' I answered, reading the box.

'It's a doll?'

'Yeah, haven't you seen the Billy doll before?'

'No,' David laughed.

What kind of man working in the gay community had never heard of Billy? Was he living under a rock? 'I have Carlos, the Latin one. You know,' I suddenly realised, 'I don't think we have the same taste in guys.'

'What do you mean?'

'I mean, if we have a threesome you're gonna want a guy that looks like a girl, a feminine type. I don't like that.'

'Not true. For me, if I play with a guy by myself, yes. That's what I'd rather have. But to play with you – doesn't matter.'

'Muscles are OK?'

'Sure,' David shrugged.

'You want to watch me get fucked by another guy. You want to watch me get used, don't you?' I teased. David smiled and nodded so I continued my taunting. 'I think we should get another guy and you should tell me what to do to him,' I whispered in his ear. 'That way you can show off what a good slave you've taught me to be.' David just continued smiling and nodding as we exited back onto Seventh Avenue.

The snow had stopped falling so we wandered at leisure down Christopher Street. While David finished his coffee and smoked a cigarette I explained that Christopher was Gay Main Street, USA. I was so busy tour guiding I walked right past The Leatherman.

'Oops! We just passed the leather store. It's back here.'

I led David through the small entrance and down the spiral staircase that was so narrow he had to turn his broad shoulders sideways to descend. Both floors were soaked in the odour of high-quality harnesses, whips and floggers. The staff were practising tops and bottoms who knew their shit and I was quite eager to talk shop, to impress my master with my own S&M knowledge. I plucked a gorgeous cat o' nine tails from a wall of hanging torture tools. 'Feel how heavy that is!' I exclaimed, handing it to David. He nodded, returning it to me as a pair of leather restraints caught his eye. 'You don't have your own?' I asked surprised.

'No, I do but I like these better,' he answered, weighing them in his strong hands. 'They're softer so they won't cause as much pain.'

'I thought you wanted to cause pain.'

'A little is good – just enough to show who's in control. But too much is bad.'

As a submissive who wasn't a masochist I breathed a sigh of relief. 'That's why I had to ask you to take off those handcuffs the other night. They were cutting into my wrists.'

'That's why I don't like handcuffs,' David quipped.

Two sales clerks – an older bald gentleman in leather vest and black jeans and a young alterna-kid in black sweater and sporting a brushed-down black mohawk – were working the slow downstairs floor. Neither gave a second glance to this possibly hetero couple in a gay leather store. Both were extremely friendly and helpful (especially the older guy when David took off his sweater to try on a latex shirt!) but what I appreciated most was that they went out of their way to include me in the conversation even though it was my beautiful buff master asking the questions.

'Do you have any bondage videos?' David asked the smitten older one. 'I want to see how to tie people up.'

'I don't think they have any straight bondage videos,' I interjected. 'Do you want gay or straight, David?'

'Straight.'

'Well, we have these two,' the clerk admitted, holding up two boxes with cheesy cover art to show me, 'but they aren't very good.'

'Let me get you the address for Extreme Video,' the alterna-kid offered. 'They should have straight bondage tapes.'

It was so relaxing shopping in a store for which kink was the norm, in which no one even blinked twice when I waved a metal double clip in the air, shouting 'I need this to fasten my restraints! Do you think it's big enough?' across the room.

David glanced over from where he was examining gags. 'Yup. As long as I can grab the whole thing with my hand.'

'You like the ball gags? I like them,' I said, joining him.

'Not really – I like blow jobs too much,' he chuckled.

'Well, you can remove it when you want one.'

'True.' David stuck the ball in his mouth then promptly spit it out. 'Yuck! I'd rather have a dildo in my mouth!'

'What are you doing putting it in your mouth?' I laughed, realising that was the leather shop equivalent of trying on underwear.

'You can't be a good top unless you try the toys out first on yourself,' David explained, wandering towards a neat row of blindfolds. 'I like to play with vision. Come over here.'

I ran to my master and he strapped several different blindfolds to my head like he was trying to fit me with the perfect pair of sunglasses. Finding a simple black one he liked David adjusted it over his own eyes before placing it on the glass display case beside the blue ball gag he'd selected.

The alterna-kid came over to hand me the address for Extreme Video. I eyed the location written on the back of a business card and laughed. 'Look, David,' I said, offering it to him.

'What?'

'Look at the address – 46th and Eighth!'

David chuckled. 'Oh, I know where that is!' he told the kid. 'I live right over there.'

I wish, I pined as my master gathered together the ball gag, blindfold, restraints and fastener. I ascended the spiral staircase then waited for David at the register. When he joined me, the cashier tallied the items and David pulled a bill from the wad of hundreds he was holding in a fanny pack around his waist. I'd never been shopping with someone who carried thousands of dollars in cash before. 'How much do you make just to dance?' I pried.

'Just dancing? Three-fifty a week – it's not very much.'

'Wow!' At five shows a day that worked out to ten bucks a show – no wonder they all hustled!

We thanked the courteous staff and hit Gay Main Street once again. As we backtracked to Seventh Avenue a window display caught David's eye. 'Socks! We have to go in there!' he cried with a little boy's enthusiasm.

I looked over to the porn store he was pointing at which featured mannequin sluts in lingerie. 'Stockings!' I corrected.

'What? Say it again.'

'Stockings.'

'Stockings,' he repeated, tasting the word on his tongue.

'Yeah.' We crossed the street and entered the sex shop. The first thing I noticed were the many children's videos they had for sale. 'Wow, you sure have a lot of kids' movies,' I told the Indian clerk.

'Yes, yes, forty percent,' he agreed in a heavy accent.

'Giuliani's guys actually come in and count to make sure?'

'No, but they do come in and look around.'

I'm sure they did. 'Unbelievable!' I exclaimed ruefully. But there was no time to chitchat about the puritanical mayor since by now David had found the stockings section and was calling impatiently for me to join him. 'Did you see the amount of children's videos they're selling?' I said to my master.

David wasn't interested in discussing Giuliani's zealotry. Ignoring my question he asked, 'Which ones do you like?'

I studied the choices – devil red, white with lace, black fishnets – but nothing caught my eye. I actually

hated stockings. 'Mmm, I don't know. You choose.'
David picked up a frilly white pair and then a black
lace one, unable to decide. 'Well, the white's submissive. But the black's slutty,' I offered.

'What?' David asked, snapping from his stocking
reverie.

'The white pair looks like it's for little girls. The
black is for sluts,' I clarified.

'I don't want little girl stockings!' David exclaimed
and returned them to the wall. Then he put back the
black as well. He pulled down a pair with 'bitch'
printed all over them. 'Here.'

He handed the package to me and I checked the
size. It was one-size-fits-all. I guess a bitch is a
bitch.

'I am so hard right now!' David shouted and, like
a kid in a candy shop, dashed off to examine a PVC
harness. 'Will this fit you?' he called.

I joined him and looked over the black harness
attached to panties ensemble. The tag said it was
one-size-fits-all. Of course. 'I think so.'

'Can you wear it?'

'I'll wear whatever my master wants,' I answered
like a good submissive.

'I know,' he said with a smile, 'but I want you
comfortable.'

'I'm comfortable in anything but tight latex,' I
replied shrugging, so David brought the harness and
stockings to the cashier. 'What are you going to do
to me tonight?' I whispered as he took another
hundred from his pack.

'None of your business,' he stated, handing the bill
to the Indian clerk.

After David got his change we left the sex shop/
kids' video store and checked the time. It was three

already and David had a show in half an hour so I walked him to Eighth Avenue as he transferred some items to one of the bags. 'OK, this is your bag. I want you wearing this tonight. Wear whatever else you want but be sure you have these on,' he directed sternly.

'Yes,' I replied demurely and he gave me a quick kiss on the lips.

'I know you've got your period, baby,' he added sweetly, hailing a cab. 'We'll just play a little. I'll call you after the last show.' And with that my master got inside a taxi that disappeared into the traffic lurching uptown.

Holding tight to the plastic bag I floated back home. Now this was my idea of romance! Entering my seventh floor walkup, I glanced inside to make sure David had remembered to give me the metal fastener for my restraints. Yup, it was there – right along with the PVC harness, bitch stockings – and five-inch butt plug! Where the hell did that come from?

I pulled out the plug and looked it over – twenty bucks from The Leatherman. I should have paid more attention at the cash register!

By half past ten I was thoroughly buzzed on an adrenaline high. I had just slid into the PVC harness and bitch stockings when David called. 'Hey, baby. Bad news.'

'What?' I asked, my heart falling to the floor.

'I got a stay-over,' he sighed. 'Some guy just gave me two thousand bucks to spend the night.'

'Oh, no.'

'I know. There's nothing I can do. It's business, baby.'

'I know, I know.' He sounded as depressed as I was so I tried to lighten things up. 'But *ho-ney*,' I purred in my finest drag queen voice, 'I look *so hot* right now!'

· David laughed, exhaling all the tension in his voice. 'No! No! Stop! I don't want to hear any more!'

I joined in the laughter until we both got caught in silence, tangled in a loss for words and not wanting to leave the line. 'Well, I guess I'll see you –'

'In June,' David told me.

'I'll make sure my roommate gets the message to me if I've moved by then.'

'Very good,' he continued in a businesslike tone.

'OK, see you then,' I said quickly about to hang up when David stopped me.

'Kisses all over your body,' he said tenderly.

'Thank you,' I replied, so very touched. 'That feels really, really good.'

I lay the receiver in its cradle as my heart began to break. This truly was the ultimate S&M relationship.

The Taming

(June 2000)

Aimee sent me an email. 'I'm a bit fascinated that someone has managed to break your spirit by dominating you physically. I wondered if there was a way to tame Lauren or if she would always be wild.'

My master arrived back in New York before I did. I had just returned from a week's vacation in San Francisco when I got the call.

'Hello, Lauren. It's David,' he said with not a hint of nervousness in his voice. 'I guess you're at work or on your way home from work. Whatever. Just wanted to let you know I'm in town. I'm staying at the Marriott. The number is 398-1900, Room 3850. So I'll wait for your call. Bye, baby,' he signed off, with the self-assured tone of an old friend, someone with whom important shared experiences had linked your lives. Strangely, in such a short time it was what he had become.

Of course I immediately called the hotel and left my master a message detailing my whereabouts then waited on edge all Thursday night for him to phone back. He never did. All Friday afternoon I tried to remind myself that he had clients to see, hard-ons to maintain, but I couldn't shake the sadness. When I got home from work my sister asked if I'd yet heard David's message on the machine.

This time his voice was quite anxious, explaining that he was calling me again because I'd never called him back. But I had! I quickly called the Marriott and got a clerk to double-check that David's voicemail was working before I left yet another message. I waited three hours before trying again. 'Hey, David!' I greeted happily when my master himself answered. 'Did you get my message?'

'I just got it.' He exhaled in relief. 'You know what happened?'

'What?'

'I have a roommate this time – this guy is staying with me. He wrote down your message, deleted it and then forgot to give it to me! I asked him, "Did some girl call for me?" and he goes, "Oh, shit!" Uh-huh!' David harrumphed.

'Well, at least I didn't leave the first message on someone else's machine by mistake! I thought I might have told some stranger that I was shopping at a fetish store before leaving my number. I was afraid some freak might call back!'

'So, baby, what are you doing tomorrow night?' David asked promptly.

'I'm going dancing,' I said dejectedly since I was eager to see him right away.

'Where?'

'Either the Polish club out by me or the Russian club by you – something Eastern-European.'

'OK, I think I would like to see you tomorrow night,' he decided.

'Not tonight?'

'I have clients and then an early show tomorrow.'

'But I shaved!' I whined impatiently.

The silence at the other end lasted so long I wondered if we'd gotten cut off until I heard, 'Where? Your pussy?'

'Uh-huh.'

'Your ass, too? Everywhere?'

'Uh-huh,' I lied.

'Hmm, maybe I can use you tonight. I'll call you back.'

'When? Tomorrow?' I asked boldly before I could swallow my sarcasm.

'No!' David laughed. 'In an hour. If I can see you, though, you will have to be a very good slave. I will tell you what to wear, what to do and what to say,' he continued, slowing every word for emphasis.

'Yes, sir.'

'Bye.'

By the time he phoned an hour later to say I would have to wait until the next night I was practically chomping at the bit. 'OK,' I sighed, my voice heavy with disappointment.

'Don't you worry,' David reassured in an effort to cheer me up. 'You will get what you deserve.'

Saturday couldn't fly by fast enough. I was running errands when David called my machine to let me know I was going to 'get it good' – and to nicely ask me to leave a message detailing what I was in the mood for that evening. I played back the recording for Roxanne.

'Oh, wow! He sounds like your boyfriend. He's so sweet! Can I have a copy of that to masturbate to?'

I laughed out loud and told her to stick with her pocket rocket then returned my master's call. 'Hey, David!' I happily exclaimed upon hearing his hello.

'I'm busy. I'll have to call you back,' he barked sourly, abruptly cutting me off.

'OK,' I said as David hung up on me to attend to his client.

When he phoned again at eight that night my sister answered. 'Lauren, it's David. He thought I was you!' Jordana shouted through giggles so I got on the line.

'Are you hitting on my sister?' I teased.

'No!' David protested, laughing. 'You have the same voice!'

'No, we don't! You were hitting on my sister, weren't you?' I continued playfully.

'Is she submissive like you?' David asked, bantering to his advantage.

'No, actually she's quite dominant.'

'No, I'm not interested – I think I like playing with you too much.'

His praise made me blush. 'What time are you working till tonight?' I inquired.

'Tree.'

'You have clients afterwards?'

'No, no clients after tree – and I already told my roommate he cannot bring anyone over after tree.'

'So, how are we going to do anything now that you have a roommate?'

'None of your business!' David snapped, making me laugh. 'You will bring all your toys and the ones that I bought you – and wear the stockings with open-toed shoes so I can see your feet.' My master commanded that I be at his hotel room at 'tree-thirty' then issued a final order. 'Call my machine as soon as you get off the phone and leave me a message telling me how submissive you're going to be for me tonight. I want to hear how well you're going to suck my cock. You'll help me do my show tonight. I'm going to call the machine right before I go onstage so I'll get a hard-on.'

'Yes, sir.'

The minute after David hung up I dialled his hotel voicemail to whisper about wearing the slutty bitch stockings while I sucked the big cock that I longed for, that I hadn't tasted in months – until call waiting interrupted my porn monologue, forcing me to click over when the beep became too distracting.

'Lauren, it's Dad. How are you? Is your sister around?'

'Uh, hold on.' Mortified, I changed lines to quickly finish worshipping my master's cock then relinquished the phone to Jordana. As soon as my sister was through talking baseball I called Roxanne, waking her from her nap so she could help me figure out how the hell to get sex toys past the thorough security check at Club Europa. I finally decided creatively to wrap up my bondage gear and five-inch butt plug like a birthday present. 'I swear to you I will never set foot inside that club again if a bouncer pulls out my butt plug,' I confided gravely to Roxanne.

By the time the Russian diva's car service arrived at my door at midnight I was head to toe butterflies. 'What are you doing?' I asked, finding Roxanne leaned against the big blue minivan talking with the driver.

'He's going to take pictures for me,' she answered happily. 'Get out of the car,' she ordered the confused South American cabby but he just sat there and smiled.

'I don't think he has time to take pictures of you. He's probably got other customers to pick up. Come on – let's just walk over to Europa. I'll take a picture along the way.'

Reluctantly Roxanne consented and let the poor guy go. I snapped two photos of her posing in her 'secretary gone bad' outfit before arriving at the club. Luckily, the Polish bouncer who liked to woo her in Russian was there and he became so busy making comrades that he forgot to check my bag. Whew!

I knew I was going to be a sweaty mess by the time I reached David's hotel room but I didn't care. The music was just too good to stop dancing, besides I needed an outlet for my overcharged libido. NYC nightclubs had been my haven since my arrival from Colorado in the late eighties – more for the sense of community than for the endless sexual possibilities. I was known as the 'gothic cheerleader' and 'Limelight girl' all the way to Boston for my unbridled dance floor enthusiasm at Communion, Limelight's Tuesday night of dark drama (especially when the Sisters of Mercy were involved). Craig 'Curiosity', my first friend in New York, ran the new wave nights at Pyramid club, where I also lip-synched with the drag queens as Lauren Vile. I learned early on that I could be anything and everything – boy, girl, both – inside the safety of a song.

But that was years ago (when Roxanne was still literally a club 'kid', sneaking out of her diplomat mom's apartment in five-inch platform boots), and the American scene had moved on to less innocent fabulousness and more cynical grunge. Thankfully, my Polish neighbourhood in Brooklyn was still stuck in the Communist eighties so it wasn't unusual to hear cheesy Modern Talking tunes mixed in with the latest club hits.

A hot guy walked by and I checked out his ass without missing a beat of 'Eisbar'. Lost in the newest trance I thought of David's hard cock longing for my lips and moments later found myself miraculously surrounded by buff men able to read my dirty mind. Even the aloof Yugoslavian (been there, done him) was looking at me – though he was probably just remembering the night he'd fucked me in the very same camouflage minidress I now had on. When Roxanne and I finally took a break to bother Andre the bartender for our usual ice water piled high with cherries I glanced at my watch to see it was nearing three. We had to leave soon if I was going to make it to my master's door on time. 'We need to go now,' I told the diva, 'or else I'll be punished for being late.'

While waiting outside for the car service, I used the pay phone to leave a message for David that I was on my way. It was already ten past and there was no way I was going to make it to his room by 'tree'-thirty – but I didn't tell him that!

Minutes later another minivan arrived to take us back over the bridge. 'No VCR?' Roxanne asked, disappointed.

'What are you talking about?' I inquired.

'The last one had a VCR. Oh, here, I almost forgot,' she said, opening her bag and handing me the copy of *Full Metal Jacket* she'd borrowed two weeks before. 'I watched it on the way over to get you.'

'They have VCRs in livery cabs now?'

'Yeah – and a bar.'

'No way! Are you sure you didn't call a limo service by mistake?'

Unable to view Kubrick's Vietnam saga on the ride into Manhattan, Roxanne asked the driver to tune the radio to KTU. 'What are you doing?' she wondered as I changed into open-toed heels.

'I may as well get a head start on my outfit!'

'Hey, can we stop to take pictures?' Roxanne shouted to the cabby.

'No!' I protested. 'I'm going to be late as it is and I'm sure this guy doesn't want to make more than two stops! I'll take a picture for you when he drops me off.'

We descended into the belly of the beast at exactly 'tree'-thirty. Roxanne and I both climbed out at 46th and Broadway where I snapped two pictures of the 'secretary gone bad' in front of an XXX palace then dashed for the Marriott. 'Hey – nice shoes!' she called after wishing me luck as I stumbled along the pavement in my submissive sandals like a drunken queen. I flipped her off before being swallowed inside the skyscraping tourist trap.

The Marriott Marquis was specifically designed to prevent its guests from realising they were staying a hop, skip and a jump away from transvestite whores and homeless heroin addicts. Consequently it was built like a fortress, to keep assorted riffraff who couldn't afford the four-hundred-dollar-per-night rooms (i.e., me) out. It took forever just to find the fucking lobby! And when I finally did arrive at the night clerk's desk he didn't want to let me in.

'Room 3850? Are they expecting you?' he asked doubtfully, eyeing my high heels and camouflage minidress, trying to determine if someone had indeed ordered a hooker.

'Yes!' I exclaimed impatiently. Didn't he realise it was twenty to four already and my punishment would only increase with my tardiness?

'What did you say your name was again?' the clerk asked as he hesitantly picked up the phone.

'Lauren,' I sighed, though I'd never given him my name in the first place.

'Oh, I'm sorry,' he apologised, setting down the receiver as instant recollection overcame his suspicion. 'I forgot. He told me you'd be coming. Go on up. 38th floor.'

I thanked the overzealous gatekeeper and got inside the glass elevator. I hit '38' and skyrocketed, Star Trek-style, to the top. Fortunately, finding David's room proved much less complicated than locating the lobby and moments later I was at my master's door. He opened it on the second knock.

'You're late!' David barked, but before I had a chance to respond he grabbed my head, thrusting passionate kisses down my throat in the doorway. 'Tongue! Give me your tongue!' I obeyed so my master could suck it into his mouth. Then he pulled me inside and ordered me to my knees. 'What are you wearing?' he asked, shaking his head in disapproval.

'I'm sorry I'm late, sir. I didn't have time to change. I have my outfit with me.'

'What is this? Army girl? You just come from a fight?' he taunted.

'No, sir.'

'You make me wait?' David shot back harshly.

'I'm sorry, sir,' I repeated, staring up at his muscular frame. He was wearing a black net shirt and blue jeans. He looked like a blue-collar god.

'Open my pants and take out my dick. I want to see how well you can suck it.' I unbuttoned his jeans and reached inside, releasing the stiff muscle from its denim confinement. David watched my mouth intently, observed his own cock disappearing further and further down the wet hole. 'That's enough,' he finally said, directing me by the hair from his protesting dick. 'Get changed.' I took my bag of goodies into the bathroom and began to undress but before I even had the chance to unwrap my fake presents I heard David's scolding voice. 'What is taking you so long?'

'I'm sorry, sir, I'm going as fast as I can,' I called, carefully slipping into my bitch stockings, bringing the sheer nylons to mid-thigh before adjusting the PVC harness and panties to a perfect fit. David yelled something indecipherable, which I ignored in my rush to buckle my white submissive sandals.

'I'M TALKING TO YOU!'

'Sorry, sir, I couldn't hear you. I'm coming out now.'

Frazzled, I gathered my empty bags like a homeless porn star, stepped out of the bathroom and rounded the corner to where David sat wide-legged on a chair in front of the television. As he looked up a wicked grin spread across his face. 'Much better. Walk around for me.' Slowly and self-consciously I moved about the room. 'Bend over. Let me see your ass.' I leaned down and looked nervously at my toes. 'Nice. Your ass is rounder this time. Better than the last time.'

I didn't think I had a board butt to begin with. 'Thank you, sir.'

'Get up.' I stood straight and stared at my master. 'You are my perfect toy.'

'Thank you, sir.' My heart soared with his sincerity.

'Come over here,' David said softly as he tapped his shoulders, signalling me to give him a massage.

Standing behind my master's chair I rubbed his broad back. 'I just want to be perfect for you,' I whispered tentatively into his ear. With head hung low David smiled but his eyes remained closed. I looked up to meet our reflections in the wide mirror on the wall – my master completely oblivious as I voyeuristically watched him take in my touch, observed him absorb me, felt myself becoming a part of him.

When David finally opened his eyes his smile was beautiful and serene. 'Now do my hands,' he told my reflection.

I walked around the chair and took David's hands in mine as he penetrated me with his gaze. I placed his index finger in my mouth and sucked slowly. 'You own me,' I said softly. He nodded. He knew.

'You are going to hurt so much tonight,' my master responded gently. 'I am going to fuck you so hard. I want to feel the difference between every hole.'

'Yes, sir.'

'First I'm going to fuck you in the mouth,' he continued gravely. 'You understand?'

'Yes, sir,' I answered naïvely. Blow job – been there done that, I thought, but I was soon to learn the enormous difference in control between sucking and getting fucked.

'I am going to come in your throat and you will swallow it – all my juice.'

'Yes, sir.'

'Good. Get down on your knees over here and open your mouth.' David gathered my long mane into a ponytail as I kneeled between his powerful thighs. 'Don't you have something to tie your hair back with?'

'No, sir.'

'Why not?'

'Um, I forgot, sir?'

'You don't forget again. I want to see your mouth on my dick.'

'Yes, sir.'

My master placed his ever-ready erection into his chosen hole. As my tongue caressed his shaft in Pavlovian response he reprimanded me sharply. 'No! Open your mouth!' Stunned, I dropped my jaw as far as it would go and before my mind could process what was happening David had grabbed the back of my head and thrust his fat cock all the way down my throat. My gag reflex kicked in. 'Come on! Use that *magic mouth*!' he taunted, throwing back in my face what I'd bragged I had that very first night we met.

For the first time in my sexual life I was at a loss as to how to please. David demanded more than any other man I'd been with. Clueless, I continued to choke until he froze in disgust and took his hard candy from my mouth.

'If you can't make me come this way then I will fuck you in the ass,' he threatened slowly and calmly. 'No lubrication. It's going to hurt. You understand?' he whispered.

'Yes, sir.'

'Good.' Helplessly I watched David rise to remove the belt from his pants. I parted my lips in obedience to his cock, letting my master have his way with my entire body as his strap came down softly on my ass. 'You leave me a message telling me how much you want my cock? Well, take it!' he exclaimed, drilling my mouth like it was a pussy.

I prayed to the sex gods that David would come before I puked as my master's cock expanded down my throat, showing no mercy even as I retched. Teary-eyed I let out a gasp of relief when he finally pulled out and waved his saliva-drenched erection in my face, releasing his heavy load with a thunderous roar.

'Go clean yourself up,' he directed tonelessly as warm cum dripped onto my PVC harness. 'Then bring out a towel and clean me up.' After wiping my face and chest I ran a towel under the bathroom faucet then returned to where David sat on the chair to gently place it on his dick. He rolled his eyes with an exaggerated slapstick-comedy groan. 'Cold!' I leapt up and dashed back to the bathroom, his laughter following me all the way. 'Where are you going?'

'I'll make it warmer.' On my second attempt I tenderly took David's cock in my hands and dabbed it dry.

'Good. Now get down on your hands and knees over there,' he ordered, pointing to a pillow and towel he'd laid on the floor. I crawled to kneel on the pillow, ass towards him, listening as he retrieved the bottle of lube from the desk, squirting the thick liquid onto his palm. Wet fingers spread my pussy lips apart, invaded my asshole then fondled my firm butt cheeks. 'I shouldn't even be doing this,' David muttered disgustedly and slapped my ass hard. 'You don't deserve this,' he continued, gently rubbing the red imprint left by his hand.

'Thank you, sir,' I said softly.

I felt David's finger inside my asshole, then two, then something a bit bigger. 'Push,' David whispered and the butt plug slid in with ease. 'Now squeeze.' Following instructions, I held the toy firmly in place. 'Good,' my master praised. 'Now go get a condom over by the bed.' On hands and knees I went to where David had set two unwrapped rubbers on the night-stand, picked up one then returned like a dog. 'Is your toy hurting you?' he inquired, genuinely concerned.

'No, sir.'

'Good. Now put the condom on with your mouth.'

Instantly David's cock lengthened between my lips. Pushing me away he whirled me back around, sending body and brain into fast-forward. David was fucking me from behind, my hands and knees burning against the carpeted floor. No. I was leaned over the bed, my master pumping my pussy and me absorbing his wild thrusts like a willing dog. No. I was bent over the back of a chair with wheels, which slid smack into the wall, my head forced into the seat cushion on impact. David's groans and my whimpers the only soundtrack until the world stopped when my master pulled the plug.

'You know what I'm going to do, don't you?' David taunted rhetorically.

'Yes, sir,' I replied automatically. David penetrated me slowly, his huge cock disciplining my asshole inch by inch. Once again my life shifted into overdrive and I somehow went from hanging over the back of a chair like a carelessly tossed coat to lying prone on the mattress, hands pinned behind. All the while my master's anal pounding became a punishment I could barely take. I gasped as he pulled out and flipped me over. I felt like a marathoner about to cross the finish line, ecstatic at my mind's ability to overcome the physical wall of pain.

'Lick my balls!' he ordered, hovering above my head, his engorged cock a time bomb threatening to explode in my face. I closed my eyes and ran my tongue along the heavy hairless sacs, the smell and taste of sweat in my nose and on my lips, as David jerked himself off – until abruptly he stopped. 'Nope.

We'll save that for later.' Then he dashed off to the bathroom. 'Break time!' he called over running water.

I was too exhausted to move. I was reminded of kickboxing of all things, when I'd hold the pads for someone much bigger and stronger than me. Even though I wasn't the one punching, the active participant, being the passive one absorbing the blows was just as exhausting. That's what sex was like with David – only without the pads between us! David returned and plopped down on the other mattress. 'We each have our own beds?' I asked, confused.

David laughed. 'No. That's my roommate's bed. This one is ours.'

'But you came all over this one!'

'No, I didn't,' David countered assuredly then paused. 'Did I?'

I checked the duvet. He was right. I was lying on a towel on the bed and he hadn't come except for the one time on my face. 'No, you're right. You didn't.' David picked up the remote control and began surfing. 'No interesting stories for me?' I asked.

David thought hard. 'No, nothing I can think of. I did have a guy who was about five or six hundred pounds this week.'

'Really? What did he want?'

'Nothing unusual. Mostly just cuddling.'

He was breaking my heart. I suddenly became infuriated with the illegality of prostitution. David could have been arrested for tenderly touching a man who might never get held like that otherwise! I recalled David telling me how he viewed his work as providing a necessary service. For some it really was.

'So, how was dancing?' David asked, changing the subject.

'The music was great. I was getting hit on left and right, though. I think all the guys must have known I was getting fucked tonight.'

'Ahh. They could feel it.' An evil smile formed on David's lips.

'I think so. And two of my former one-night-stands were there.' He laughed with surprise. 'So, where's your roommate?' I wondered.

'He got paid fifteen hundred dollars tonight – to fuck a girl even!'

'Really? He's that hot?' I asked, getting excited.

'No, no. He's just lucky. Some gay guy wants to watch him fuck his wife.'

'Wow! Do you get that, too?'

'I haven't yet.' David shook his head sadly.

'Why do you have a roommate this time?'

'It's too expensive in New York in the summer so when this guy called me up and asked if I wanted to share a room I told him to book it.'

'You don't know him?'

'Not really. He's some Hungarian guy. I don't really like him. None of the dancers this time have any sense of humour. I hate sharing a room.' I removed my PVC outfit and crawled naked into bed beside David. 'What movie do you want to watch?'

I looked through the choices displayed on the television screen. Only *Fight Club* and *The Sixth Sense* were watchable. '*Fight Club*,' I picked.

'I've seen it.'

'So have I. Wasn't it good?'

'It was OK.'

'It's better than all the other choices. Plus, it's a David Fincher film with Brad Pitt. It'll be just like *Se7en* only not in French!'

David honoured my request and we settled in to watch the movie.

'My lips are numb.'

'What?' David asked, bewildered.

'I just realised my lips and tongue are numb. Probably from the condoms.'

'I hate these condoms.'

'I hate nonoxynol-nine. It makes your lips go numb.'

'It does?'

'Haven't you ever sucked cock before?'

'Yeah,' David answered matter-of-factly.

'Then you should know what I'm talking about.'

As the credits for *Fight Club* appeared I started to get sleepy so I rolled over and closed my eyes. As I began to drift off David leaned over to sweetly plant a kiss on my lips. 'Goodnight,' he whispered.

'Goodnight.'

Seconds away from being lulled into a deep slumber by Brad Pitt I heard the door open.

'Hey!'

'Hey,' David replied. 'How was your night?'

'Good. How'd you do today?'

'A thousand.'

'That's good.'

'Yes, but it hasn't been a lucky week for me. I've had to work very hard for my money.'

'Uh-huh.'

'What is that?'

'Caesar salad with grilled chicken.'

'Can I have some?'

'No, man. I'm starving. Order your own. What are you watching?'

'*Fight Club*. You seen it?'

'Yeah. It's good.'

'You're going to eat all of that?'

'Yeah, bro. I haven't eaten all day. Order one. Here's the number.'

Exasperated, I sat up in bed. I looked at the roommate. He was tall, dark – and of course, buff and gorgeous.

'Hey!' He nodded at me.

'Hey.' I turned to David. 'I can't sleep.'

'Then watch the movie,' David suggested, then dialled for delivery.

Resigned to the fact that I wasn't going to get any rest with the Hungarian and French accents being tossed back and forth like the stripper's Caesar salad, I decided to throw my American voice in as well. 'So, did you get to fuck a girl?' I asked, making small talk.

'Nope.' The Hungarian shook his head as he stuffed salad into his mouth.

'A guy?'

'I don't fuck guys!' he shot back. Oops. I'd forgotten. Rule number one – asking a straight hustler if he fucks guys is like asking him if he fucks his mother.

'But you got paid anyway?' I tried soothingly.

'Yup.'

'Well, that's good.'

'What did you do tonight?' the Hungarian asked David after he'd placed his order with the diner.

'I had a client, rented a sex movie while I was waiting for her, fucked her in the mouth and now we're watching *Fight Club*.' David flashed me a demon grin. I had definitely entered the boys' territory, complete with locker-room bravado.

'You rented a sex movie?' the Hungarian asked like he'd just found his big brother's stash of *Playboys*.

'Yeah.'

'How was it?' he continued wide-eyed.

Hell – this guy just got hired to fuck some gay guy's wife in front of him and he was shocked that David had rented a porno?

'It was OK.' I lay back down and closed my eyes again. The phone rang. 'Yeah?' David answered. He listened. 'I'm sleeping,' he finally said into the receiver and hung up.

The Hungarian picked up the phone. 'Hello? Did the order for the Marriott Marquis go out yet? No? Can you put a piece of strawberry cheesecake in with that?'

'*Way*! Chocolate, too!' David added.

'And a piece of chocolate cheesecake, too. Thank you.' No sooner had he disconnected then the phone rang a second time. I dragged the duvet over my spinning head as the Hungarian chatted with a client. Finally, David turned off the lights and I was alone with Brad Pitt once again. For about two minutes. A light clicked back on. Drawers opened then closed.

'Why do you have to make so much noise?' David barked.

'Sorry.'

'And why do you have the light on?'

'I'm going to take a shower, bro.'

'Well, you don't need the light on to take a shower, bro!' David snapped sarcastically.

'Sorry.' The bathroom light switched back off but now I really couldn't sleep. He was going to take a shower? Discreetly, I removed the blanket from my face and, feigning closed eyes, tried to catch a glimpse of the Hungarian's naked torso in the light of the television set. To add to the titillation, I even let the white sheets slide seductively off my own bare body to see if he would notice me. David, however, was the only one to notice – and he promptly covered me back up.

I managed to get a glimpse of muscle before there was a knock at the door. David leapt from the bed like Superman then threw on his jeans to receive his food. He returned to bed and began munching away. The Hungarian finished his shower and wrapped a towel securely around his waist. I finally fell fast asleep.

The phone rang early in the afternoon. 'Yeah? Gabe!' David handed off the receiver to the Hungarian.

'Hi, Jay. No, no problem. Come at two.' He hung up. 'Hey,' Gabe said to David, 'I've got a client at two.'

'I heard!' David snapped.

'What time is it?' I asked groggily.

'One-fifteen,' David said.

'Arrgh.' I sat up and slyly watched as Gabe put on his pants and went into the bathroom.

'You want to go get breakfast?' David asked me.

'I want to suck your cock,' I teased.

'Then suck it.'

Exposed above the covers, I licked the head of David's appreciative dick, slowly running my tongue up the shaft to taste the luscious balls – better than breakfast. David groaned contentedly until I stopped when I heard Gabe return from the bathroom.

'What are you doing?' David asked me.

'Your roommate,' I protested.

'So? Suck.'

I took David's growing cock in my mouth and he brought the duvet over my head, making no other attempt to conceal the debauchery going on. On the contrary he began to delve deeper down my throat, softly moaning his dirty pleasure. As my wet mouth danced to the rhythm of his thrusts, I wondered if David just didn't care who witnessed his blow jobs or if he was antagonistically reminding the Hungarian that he'd gotten pussy and Gabe hadn't. My wrist restraints were still in plain view on the nightstand. David had fucked me on a towel on top of the poor guy's bed. Definitely a case of hardcore *machismo*, I concluded.

I could hear Gabe gathering his things together as David's cock elongated, filling my mouth with his penetrating flesh. 'You leaving?' David asked.

'Yeah. I'm going out.'

'Good.' The minute Gabe was out the door David tugged me by the hair off his huge dick. 'I'm going to fuck you.'

David took the other unwrapped condom off the nightstand and quickly rolled it on, then harshly dragged me on top, forcing his anxious cock inside my non-lubricated pussy. Pain shot all the way up to my bladder and I let out a cry but David only rammed harder with every whimper, moving my immobile hips for me. Shoving me aside, he threw my legs above my head, single-handedly gangbanging my sore hole until I was moments away from crying mercy. He pushed me onto my side then came with an earthshaking moan inside my still tight pussy. When the world stopped spinning, David went into the bathroom, returning with a warm towel for me.

'You hungry?' he asked as I washed up. 'You want to go to breakfast?'

'OK,' I replied in a daze. While David showered, I dressed then collected all my sex toys that were strewn haphazardly around the room. I was searching for the clip to my wrist restraints when David emerged fresh and clean. 'Did you have more work done?' I asked as he towel-dried his gym-built back and ass.

He whirled around to face me. 'What?'

'Your back. The tattoo.'

'The flowers are new.'

'I thought so. Do you know where my clip for the restraints went?'

'It was on the table last night. It's not there?'

'No.' David hunted for the errant clip while he put on a soft yellow cotton shirt and creaseless tan linen pants. Then he brought the strap that had punished my ass through his belt loops. He looked sharp and classy while I felt like a cheap slut in my minidress. With my smoke-filled hair and smeared make-up there was no mistaking what I'd been up to all night. 'Well, if you find it just save it for me for next time,' I said, giving up. 'It's not like I use it with anyone but you. Hey – this is yours, David,' I added, removing a bottle of Astroglide that he'd placed in my bag.

'I know.'

'You don't want it?'

'No.'

I tossed the lube back in. Before I'd met David I'd had no idea there were so many different brands on the market. Goodbye KY.

I lounged on the bed, staring at the television as David tidied up the room. During an infomercial David mimicked the announcer while tossing out garbage. 'OK. Let's go!' he finally exclaimed.

'I peeked out the window while you were in the shower to check out the view from your room,' I disclosed as, encased in glass, we beamed down to the lobby. 'You are definitely in the ugliest part of the city.'

'This hotel is like a bus station. I hate New York,' he sighed before abruptly stopping in front of the revolving door to let an elderly couple pass through first. I nearly ran straight into him.

'Well, I would hate New York, too, if this was all I saw!' I exclaimed as David picked up the pace, forcing me to trot just to keep up.

Once seated at a crowded diner on Eighth Avenue, David drank his latte and I sipped coffee while scanning the breakfast (all day) menus. It was two in the afternoon, still morning in sex industry time. David pointed at my empty cup as a Latin busboy walked by with a pot of java. A moustached waiter arrived to take our order. I began to wake up.

'So, why don't you ever spend more than a week in New York?' I asked after our food had arrived.

'Because I hate New York,' David grumbled, then dove into his huge platter of French fries, bacon and toast.

'You don't even know New York! You only know midtown!' I protested, biting into the only thing on the menu not drenched in grease or that hadn't formerly grazed on four legs – a bagel. David ignored me in favour of food so I let the subject drop. I tried to remind myself that I knew when we first met that a long-distance sex affair was what I was getting into. 'You need any money?' I stupidly offered instead as David flipped through wads of hundreds in search of smaller bills. He rolled his eyes at me dismissively. After David had paid the check we exited back into the sticky summer heat.

'I've got to go back to the hotel before my show. Where are you going?'

'Home. This way.' I motioned downtown.

'OK. Then I'll leave you.'

David took me in his arms and I clung to him fiercely, my hands around his neck like an insecure child. 'When will I see you again?'

'I don't know when I'll be back,' he answered breezily. Was he getting a rise out of keeping me guessing? I didn't doubt it for a minute. 'I'm going to call you tonight,' he added with a brief kiss before we parted. Once again I tried to tell myself that I knew what I was getting into when we first met. The reality was I hadn't the faintest clue.

The Exam

(September 2000)

I had just returned home from a lazy day of hanging out with Derek and since I wasn't expecting my master to call on a Monday the French-accented voice on the machine took me by surprise.

'Hey, Lauren. It's David. Just want to let you know I'm in town. I'm staying at the apartment on 49th Street. I'll call back a little later to give you the number. Hope everything is going well with you and your sister. I'll talk to you later. Bye.' An hour later the phone rang. 'How are you?' David asked, sounding giddy when I answered.

'Good. How are you?'

'Very, very good.'

'And why is that?' I cooed playfully.

'Because it's been a long time since I've talked to you and now I hear your voice.'

'Well, it's nice to hear from you as well!' I exclaimed, flattery getting him everywhere. 'What have you been up to?'

'I spent the summer in Montreal. I bought a business.'

'What kind of business?'

'Beauty place. Tanning, waxing, that sort of thing.'

'That's cool. Who's running it while you're in New York?'

'I have a partner. He takes care of things while I'm away.'

'So you'll keep stripping?'

'Of course! I'll have to. How else will I keep my mistress?' he slowly teased.

I laughed like a blushing schoolgirl. 'So you want to see me tonight?'

'Yes, I think I would like to beat you a bit tonight,' David answered smoothly.

'You want me to shave my pussy?' I asked demurely.

David groaned, his hard-on growing. 'Mmm, of course. Is one-thirty OK?'

'Sure, but I have to work tomorrow. I'll need to stay over.'

'No problem! I'll call you later, baby.'

I showered, letting the razor linger over my labia until all the pubic hair had rinsed down the drain with my dominant pride. Then I got all dolled up for my master in high heels and a thigh-revealing silver dress. I packed an overnight bag with office clothes for work the next day. Then I waited. And waited. And waited.

At two-thirty in the morning I got undressed and unpacked, simultaneously disappointed and furious. If I was going to get stood up for a client the least he could have done was call! But in that same instant I realised that this was typical of my master – I was his slave to be used at his convenience. Sex toys didn't merit common courtesy. At three-thirty in the morning I finally drifted off to sleep, unsure if I was angrier with David or myself for letting him so deep inside both my mind and body.

The next day I was cranky from five hours' sleep – and it didn't help that I'd gotten my period. I was in the foulest of moods.

After returning from my office temp job in Jersey City, I relaxed in a long hot bath then got ready for bed, finally falling asleep around nine-thirty. An hour and a half later the ringing phone startled me awake but I let my sister answer it.

'Lauren! It's David!'

Dazed, I fumbled to get the receiver to my ear. 'Hello?'

'Hey, baby. What are you doing?'

'I just got my period so I'm lying down.'

'Ahh. Then I will have to exploit you in a different way tonight.'

'Tonight? What happened to last night?' I asked lightly, still sore from being snubbed.

'I had clients until tree in the morning. I called but no one picked up.'

'The phone didn't ring last night,' I challenged.

'Well, I called but no machine picked up,' he lied.

'Well, you must have called the wrong number.' I decided to let the subject drop, the singsong of his French accent luring me in like a fish on a reel. 'What time tonight?'

'One or one-thirty.'

'No later?'

'No, I won't go any later. Is that OK?'

'Yeah,' I relented with a yawn. David had me in the palm of his dominant hand – and he knew it.

'Hey!' David exclaimed, like he'd just gotten a brainstorm. 'Can I rape you tonight?'

That threw me. Still half asleep I was in no condition to ponder the concept of consensual rape. 'Uh, yeah, I guess.'

'OK, baby. I'll call you later then.'

'Bye.' This time I was not rushing to get ready. I took my time leisurely tracing my eyes in black liner and was brushing out my long brown hair when David called back – at twelve-thirty.

'Hey, baby.'

'You're finished already?' I asked, startled.

'Yup, I finished early.'

'Well, I'm not dressed yet.'

'You need to get dressed to get undressed?'

'Yeah, I need about twenty more minutes. Is that OK?'

'Sure, take your time.'

I threw on my silver slip of a dress, applied lipstick and called for a car service. Then I phoned David to let him know I was on my way but the machine picked up. 'Leave your name and number and what you're calling about after the beep.' I left a message and five minutes later was out the door.

I began to get nervous as we drove into Manhattan. I couldn't stop thinking about being 'raped'. I'd never really had what I would call a 'rape fantasy'. Bondage, yes. Being completely controlled by a man, most definitely. But these were fantasies of submission. Rape involved struggle, didn't it? Was I supposed to fight him off tonight? How could I be a good submissive and fight him at the same time? And, more importantly, I was honestly afraid to battle David. I knew he would never hurt me as long as I let him do whatever he wanted (and even then he had me yelling 'mercy' most of the time) – but if I fought him? I feared I might accidentally get physically hurt.

David was into rough sex anyway. Could I take it any rougher?

I was about to find out. As I paid the driver and stepped from the car at 49th Street between Eighth and Ninth, I noticed five teenage delinquents hanging out and smoking pot on the stoop next door to David's building. The street was completely empty and I didn't like how they were eyeing my high heels and bare legs. I rang David's buzzer then waited for several minutes that seemed like hours. Where was he?

When I was finally buzzed in I quickly ascended the stairs to the vaguely familiar second floor then followed the scent of marijuana to a half-open door, which suddenly swung open to reveal my master wearing nothing but black net pants. He pulled me inside, groaning as he gently guided my head down to his crotch. Pressing my face into his half-erect cock he held it there for a few seconds, letting me absorb the scent of sweat and sex, before tugging me back up and motioning me into the bedroom. Then he left, shutting the door behind me.

Voices emanated from the living room. But he'd told me he was done with clients for the night! He must have picked up an extra trick at the last minute. Sighing, I took out my bondage gear and butt plug and laid them neatly on the floor. Moments later David returned, flinging open the door. 'Why didn't you tell me you had a client?'

'I don't. There's no client here,' David answered mysteriously as he led me into the living room. Then who just left? I wondered but didn't ask as I sat down on a cushioned chair, watching happily as David tidied the room, muscles bulging even more than the last time I saw him. He looked so incredibly hot I couldn't stop staring, my eyes burning holes into his rippling abs. He turned and smiled. And kept smiling at me. 'What?' I finally asked bashfully.

'I am just very happy to see you.'

'Me, too,' I gushed stupidly.

'Yeah?' he asked, searching my eyes to see if I meant it.

'Yeah,' I answered truthfully.

'Well, good,' David stated, switching sex movies in the VCR. Then he walked to where I self-consciously sat and pushed aside my short dress to caress my bare leg. 'Ahh. My perfect toy.' I blushed. 'So, have you been a good girl or a bad girl?' he asked, heading to the refrigerator for some water.

'A bad girl.'

'Oh, a bad girl?' David proclaimed, intrigued. 'Any new experiences?'

'Yes. I had two guys.'

'And how was it?'

'Well, I wish it was with you,' I answered honestly.

David smiled smugly. 'So what was the problem? No domination?'

'No.'

'Why not?'

'Because you're my master.'

David continued grinning cockily. 'Bad sex?'

'Well, it was with two brothers so they didn't touch each other.'

'Oh.'

'So what about you? Any new experiences?' I asked, anxious to switch the spotlight onto him.

David hesitated before responding. 'Uh, yeah.'

'Really? What?'

Taking a deep breath, he crossed to the other side of the room. 'I have a new boyfriend.'

'You do?' I inquired, trying to appear as cool as possible while my heart skipped a beat.

'Yup – but my girlfriend doesn't like him. And he has a girlfriend who I don't really like. So we're like two couples together but it's weird.'

Now it was my turn to take a deep breath. My stomach was in knots. Boyfriend. Girlfriend. Relax. Grab onto one relationship and go with it. Focus.

'So what is your boyfriend like? A top? A bottom?'

'He's a top with girls and a bottom with me.'

'Really? Is he buff?' Maybe I could use this boyfriend thing to my advantage.

'Yeah. He's a little bit smaller than me.'

'What does he look like? Cute? My type?'

'Well, he's –' David stopped and nodded over to the refrigerator. 'That's him.'

I rose to get a closer look at the photos hanging on the fridge that I had first assumed belonged to the owner of the apartment. One picture was of a standard-issue buff white guy grinning. Another showed a pretty brunette with a flower in her hair smiling sweetly at the camera.

'Is this your girlfriend?'

'Yeah.'

I took yet another deep breath. Where did these people come from? And why was he telling me about them now?

'Well, your boyfriend's kind of cute. You should bring him with you sometime for a threesome.'

'No!' David snapped, startling me. 'That's my private life!'

Now I was hurt as well as confused. 'Well, it's not like we're not friends,' I said quietly.

David softened. 'No, I know we're friends. But it doesn't matter – you'll never meet him. He's in Montreal. You know what? I'm starving,' he suddenly said, changing the subject we shouldn't have been on in the first place.

'You want to go get something to eat?'

'You hungry?'

'No, but I'll go for a walk with you.' I most definitely needed the air.

David dressed and we headed out into the balmy Indian summer night. The gang of guys was still chilling on the stoop next door but this time they looked away when they saw me. At a deli on Eighth Avenue David ordered something on a croissant then came back over to where I waited. 'You are wearing too much perfume,' he scolded.

'Sorry,' I apologised, though I really didn't give a shit. An overabundance of perfume was the least of my worries at the moment.

'It's OK. I like your perfume. You just have on too much.'

'It'll wear off,' I noted dryly.

'You don't want anything to eat?'

'No, I just got my period. My stomach isn't doing so well.'

'I'm starving!' David repeated as he paid for his sandwich and a Slim-fast bar.

'Why? Didn't you have time to eat today?'

'Yes. I ate a lot. I eat five or six times a day. But I'm still hungry.'

'Food and sex all day long, huh?'

'Uh-huh.' David laughed as he tore into his protein bar.

'So you like your new business?' I inquired on our way back.

'Yup. Gives me something to do besides think about sex all day.' David paused. 'Well, I still think about sex all day.'

'Must be nice knowing so many people into open relationships. Your girlfriend sleeps with other guys, too?'

'No. She doesn't want to. But she knows what I do.'

Somehow I doubted that she knew he had been fucking the same woman whenever he came to New York for nine months now. But I didn't say anything. That was his business, too.

'Maybe I've got to stop screwing all these Eastern European guys,' I hypothesised. 'They're too straight.'

'The French and the Italian are the best.'

'Yeah, but the Italians are crazy,' I added, thinking of my ex-lover Marco. 'I used to sleep with an Italian who lives a couple blocks from here. He's nuts.'

'Yeah, they are crazy,' he conceded, then let us into the apartment building.

Once inside the apartment I lay on the couch to watch the porno that was still playing while David unwrapped his sandwich. He scooted my feet over so he could sit down, too. 'What the hell is this?' I asked. Two guys in Halloween masks were fucking some chick on top of a racecar. 'A new genre – horror porn?'

'I guess. It's a new vari –' David stopped, swallowed and tried again. 'Vari – how do you say that word?' he asked, looking at me with curiosity.

'Variation?' I guessed.

'Yeah, variation. The box said something about sex in cars. This is not sex in cars.' David shook his head sadly.

'No. This is truly weird.' I made a mental note to remember the title for Roxanne.

David finished his meal, releasing a heavy sigh. 'Ahh! I just finished my day.' He got up and began to search around.

'What are you doing?'

'Looking for my rolling papers.'

David scoured the room until finding them in his big black suitcase. 'What if I came to the Gaiety to see you dance? Would you be mad?' I asked as he sat down to roll.

David shrugged. 'What do I care? But I can't really spend any time with you there. I'm busy when I'm at work.'

'I think the Gaiety is very sexy. It's like walking into a maximum security men's prison where the inmates are all gorgeous. You know what my problem with normal sex is?'

'What?'

'It's like junk food. It's a quick high but it doesn't fill me up for as long as S&M does. Like with S&M I feel satisfied for a longer period of time.'

David looked up from his tobacco. 'Really?' he asked surprised. 'That's like ecstasy. If I fuck on ecstasy I don't need to fuck right away again.'

'Yeah, I guess so. I guess S&M is like a drug for me. But that's bad then.'

'Why?'

'Because then I'll get addicted and want it all the time.'

'Well, then I guess you'll have to find a partner for that,' he replied pragmatically.

'Yeah, but it's hard. Most guys don't know what to do with me. I think I should come with a book of instructions.'

David laughed. 'Write one.'

The number of translations alone would make something like that impractical. I was an international slut. 'Well, it's hard to explain to guys what I want. There are a lot of issues involved here. I mean, the reason I like S&M is because it's a way for me to not be a girl. I become an object, something that you use and thus a part of you. It's like I'm absorbed into you. I come through you.'

I paused, waiting for David to look at me like I literally must have been fucked senseless somewhere along the line. 'I know,' he said nonchalantly still focused on rolling tobacco.

'What do you mean, you know?' I wondered, surprised.

'I know,' he repeated.

'You know what? That I come *through* you?'

'Yup – that's your trip.'

'Oh.'

'You ever come with guys?' David asked.

'I always come with guys,' I answered, startling him instead.

'You do?'

'Yup. I come with every guy *except* you. But the sex is better with you. I can have an orgasm with a guy or I can give myself one alone. There's nothing special about that. I need more. I have to do S&M if I want to come through a guy and most guys don't know how to let me come through them. You know, I only fuck guys I would want to be,' I added.

Briefly David looked up in surprise, taking a few puffs of his cigarette before setting it down. 'OK, I'm ready. I want you down on the floor on all fours.' Guiding me by the hair to the middle of the living room he pushed me forward, my face pressed to the carpet, ass held high in the air. Then he left the room.

He was gone an awfully long time. Upon hearing something crash to the ground, I turned to peek just as my master returned. 'Why are you looking? Curious?' he scolded as he approached. Nervously, I looked away. David lifted up my skirt and brought down my black lace panties like he was feverishly unwrapping a present. I'd forgotten I was wearing a pantiliner until he ripped it out of my lingerie, disgustedly tossing it aside.

'Curious?' he asked again as his belt hit my right ass cheek.

'Yes, sir. Sorry, sir.'

'You'd better be.' His fingers slowly dove one by one into my freshly shaved pussy. 'Look at that perfect little pussy!' David praised.

'Thank you, sir.' His strong hands inspected my firm buttocks, pinching and slapping both cheeks. 'Thank you, sir,' I repeated respectfully as David's belt caressed the left cheek with a single lash. With a heavy sigh David drenched my reddened skin in cold lube, massaging it into my exposed pussy and tight asshole. Then he got down on his knees and rammed his big latex-covered cock inside me.

It hurt like hell. I was sore from my period and David's dick felt enormous inside my wet pussy. I could tell his cock was at its full porn-star size the moment he thrust it inside me. As I whimpered like a wounded dog David drilled deep and hard, bringing my head up by the hair. He let go and my head dropped. Taking me by the rein of my hair he tugged back once again. 'I want a proud dog!' David ordered. 'Be proud.'

I continued to release small cries as I struggled to keep my chin up while David manoeuvred me onto my 'hind legs', screwing his bitch in an ever more painful position. He pulled out and dragged me over to the couch by the hair. I didn't dare turn around as he left the room but waited serenely, a pillar of strength in my ability to take so much of a man.

I knew David had returned only when I heard him place some items on the nearby table then felt his presence loom from above. He brought my head back. 'Open your mouth! Wide!' The moment my lips parted David spit then thrust his still-hard cock to the back of my throat. 'Keep it open!' he commanded, fucking my mouth while I gagged. When his insatiable cock grew tired of that willing orifice David then bent me over the couch on my rug-burned knees.

Lubed fingers probed my asshole soon to be replaced with David's favourite toy. 'Push! Now squeeze!' he ordered, expertly sliding the butt plug into place. 'Good girl,' David praised then forced his ever-ready cock inside my pussy yet again. I heard only my own moans as David penetrated deeper, still not satisfied until his dick was in my ass. He removed the butt plug, making me take what was real. My cries grew louder as David drilled my tight hole until I was on the verge of begging for mercy. 'Come on, baby. We're almost there,' he whispered tenderly in my ear. Instantly, my desire to please him overwhelmed the pain.

Wielding his dick like a weapon David sodomised me like he would never orgasm, like he would torture my ass forever. 'Mercy!' I finally cried.

David stopped – for all of two seconds. 'No, bitch! No mercy! I told you I was going to rape you,' he explained, pounding my hole even harder. He pulled out with a primal scream, roaring and convulsing and every time I thought he was through coming he would make like a lion again.

Finally, with a sigh of relief he went into the bathroom. 'I'm going to take a shower. You want one?' he called out.

'No, I'm fine,' I answered, dazed, as I dragged my spent body onto the couch and tried to collect my thoughts. I noticed my breasts were hanging out of the top of my dress and wondered when that had happened. 'I think you are the loudest guy I've ever been with in my life!' I yelled with a chuckle.

Peeking out from the bathroom David laughed heartily. '*Everybody* tells me that!'

'Well, it's true.'

'People are always like –' he slowed down his words for emphasis. '– "*What the hell was that?*"'

I giggled in agreement. 'You roar.' I curled up like a cat on the couch to watch the horror porn while David showered. He changed the videotape upon returning to the living room. 'What are you putting on?'

'*Se7en*.'

But when Jean-Claude van Damme appeared on the screen I became confused. 'This isn't *Se7en*!'

'I know,' David laughed. 'I'm joking!'

I admitted that I knew he was coming into town when I turned on the TV the week before to find *Se7en* playing. This made David laugh even harder. 'So do all girls like being fucked in the ass?' I wondered aloud as he towelled his bulging biceps.

'Uh – I don't know,' he answered, like he'd never pondered the question before. 'I guess so. I fuck everybody in the ass. I like it.'

'I didn't ask if *you* like it! I know *you* like it!'

'Yeah, I guess they all like it.'

'I thought maybe I just liked it because I'm a gay boy inside.'

'That's not what most gay men want,' he corrected.

'It's not?'

'Nope.'

'Yes it is!' I argued.

'No it's not!' David answered firmly. 'You know how many clients I have that want that?'

'How many?'

'Out of forty-tree clients, tree.'

'That's it?'

'Yup.'

That was an eye opener – personally, I couldn't see paying two hundred bucks and not getting penetrated. David picked up a pair of camouflage briefs that were lying next to the couch and tossed them to me.

'A client brought me those. He brings me a different pair to wear every time I see him.'

'How funny. What are you? G.I. Joe?' David chuckled but the underwear got me thinking. 'You have the uniform to go with it? Like from your army days?'

'No way! I threw that out!' David exclaimed self-consciously.

'Why? That is so sexy!' David rolled his eyes before taking a seat to roll a cigarette. 'Am I your only slave?' I asked sleepily.

'Yes. I used to have another.'

'Guy or girl?'

'Girl.'

'What happened to her?'

'I got rid of her when I met you.'

'Why? Because I suck cock better?'

'I just got tired of her. I don't need to have sex just to have sex. Like you're the only one I see when I come to New York. I could go over to Flashdancers and pick up a stripper but what's the point? I'd rather come here, see you, and if you're not around I have my pornos. I don't need boring sex. It's like you told me. You want someone with attitude or not at all. You saw it in my eyes.'

'Yup. You came up to me that first night at the Gaiety and looked me up and down like you were admiring a piece of meat.'

David laughed and his face suddenly lit up – eureka! 'So that's it! I wondered why I scare girls all the time.'

'Well, yes – you're very obvious. But that's a turn-on for me. If you want to fuck me don't pretend you want to date me.'

'That's what I like about you,' David stated with admiration. 'There's no bullshit.'

'Right. But then why did you pick me up?' I probed like a curious child. 'You just told me you don't need to pick up girls in New York.'

'I saw it in your eyes,' he said matter-of-factly.

'What?'

'The same thing you saw in mine.'

'That I wanted to fuck you? I looked at you like you were a piece of meat?'

'Uh-huh.'

I laughed – funny how we both liked playing the sex object to be used. 'Yeah, I guess I'm not too subtle either. Roxanne tells me that all the time.'

'Come on,' David directed, rising to motion me into the bedroom.

As soon as I stood up I realised the apartment was freezing from the air conditioning. My teeth started chattering. 'Cold! Cold!' I cried, pogo-ing to keep warm in the bedroom while David went to the kitchen to retrieve an ice pack for his aching back.

'Well, why didn't you say something before?' He grabbed a sweatshirt from the closet and tossed it at me.

128

'Thanks!' After taking off my silver dress I slipped the big grey sweatshirt over my head then promptly jumped under the covers. David joined me, setting the ice pack on the nightstand. He pulled me close, rubbing my arms to generate warmth as my teeth continued clicking. 'This is ridiculous!' I shouted.

When my temperature began to rise, David lay down on his stomach, the ice pack melting on his lower back. I let my fingers linger up and down his solid calves and thighs, over his smooth butt, alternating the tender massage of my hands with the hungry licking of my tongue.

'That's what I never get to do to you,' I whispered while squeezing the two hard globes of flesh that formed his buttocks.

'What?'

'Seduce you. I'm very good at seduction,' I cooed.

'Ahh. A side I haven't seen before?'

'Uh-huh,' I said in a singsong, wanting to climb inside his skin, get inside his head. 'So do your boyfriend and girlfriend know you have a slave in New York?' I pried.

David's muscles tightened against my question. 'No.'

'Why not? Would they be mad?' I wondered curiously.

'I don't know,' David shot back sharply.

'Well, who knows about me?' I tried. 'No one?' Did I exist outside his mind?

'I have certain clients who know about you,' he conceded with a sigh.

That seemed odd but then I supposed regulars were regulars whether you were a hooker or a hairdresser. I decided to let the subject drop before David became one big mound of tense flesh in need of a giant ice

129

pack. My eyes were growing heavy anyway so I finished the rubdown and turned over to go to sleep. David returned his ice to the nightstand then crawled under the blanket with me. 'Don't be stealing the covers from me now,' I warned.

'I don't steal covers.'

'Yes, you do. You steal everything. Covers, pillows –'

'I do?'

'Yup. No one's told you that before?'

'No. Maybe it's just when I'm away from home,' David guessed. 'There are never enough blankets and pillows.'

'Or maybe it's just with me.'

'Yes. I just want you to get closer.'

'You are so full of shit!' We both laughed sleepily and within minutes were out like two lights. Though the alarm had been set for eleven the ringing of the phone woke me from a sound rest at ten. I tried to go back to sleep while the machine picked up but the phone promptly rang again – and again. 'What the hell?' I asked, frustrated. David dragged me close, my naked body his last defence from reality before reluctantly reaching for the receiver.

'Hello? What? Is it *morning*?' he asked confused, then chuckled. 'Oh. Am I *horny*?' I climbed on top of David, tugging at the tiny nipples on his waxed chest. 'No, that's fine. I just woke up. Give me ten minutes.' David hung up, exhaling a groan of pleasure. 'Stop it.'

'Why?'

'Because it's morning.'

'Because it's morning?'

'Yeah. I've got to get up for a client.'

'And what am I supposed to do?' I pouted.

'Stay here. Go back to sleep.'

'But I've got to get ready to go to work,' I protested.

'So?' David shrugged. 'It'll take me fifteen minutes.'

'But what if he can't come in fifteen minutes?'

'Then I kick him out,' he answered on his way into the bathroom.

'David, I'm not going to be able to go back to sleep,' I called. 'Why don't I just take a shower and you put him in here?'

'You want that?' David asked, returning to the bedroom. 'Doesn't matter to me.' He brought me a towel and turned on the hot water tap. 'You're showering first?'

'No, you can go,' I offered, gathering my hair up onto the top of my head.

'I'm not taking a shower,' David said, confused.

It took me a minute to figure out he was asking if showering was the first part of my morning routine so he'd know whether to shut off the faucet. 'I'll shower first,' I clarified, surprised by his courteousness.

David left me in the bathroom just as the intercom rang, closing the door behind him. I had just stepped out of the tub and was brushing my teeth when David bolted back in, making a beeline for the toilet paper. 'He's finished.' I responded with the 'thumbs up' sign since I had a mouthful of toothpaste as David left once again. But minutes later he was back. 'Take that,' he ordered, motioning to my make-up bag on the toilet seat cover. 'Come.'

'I need to take my other stuff, too?'

'No. He just needs to use the bathroom.'

David escorted me to the living room where I plopped onto the couch with a heavy sigh. Then he drew the makeshift divider (a hanging sheet that separated the living room from the rest of the apartment that I hadn't even noticed before) closed. I waited silently, eavesdropping on the muffled voices by the front door then the sound of kisses being exchanged on both cheeks.

'Sorry about that, baby,' David apologised, pulling back the curtain.

'You have another client at eleven?'

'No, that was him – he was early.' I returned to the bathroom to finish readying myself for another boring workday, and emerged to find David devouring a bowl of cereal in front of the television, fixated on *The Maury Povich Show*. 'This is crazy!' he cried as one trailer park diva accused another of 'messing with her man'.

'Oh, come on! You don't have white trash TV in Canada?'

'What?'

'White trash TV,' I repeated. 'This stuff.'

'No. I've never seen shows like this before,' he stated, wide-eyed.

'Pretty stupid,' I opined. 'I mean, who cares if some guy slept with more than one woman? I just don't get this monogamy thing. It seems so silly.'

'Not everyone can separate mind and body,' David ventured.

'Well, you don't have to necessarily separate the two. You just have to realise that people can do and feel different things for different people,' I suggested, pouring myself a glass of water. As I headed for the couch and a better view of David's bemused face, he stopped me.

'Over here,' David ordered, pointing to the floor between his knees, his eyes never wavering from the television screen. 'Suck my dick.'

'Your client just sucked your dick.'

'I know. But I didn't come. Suck it,' he repeated, holding his soft member with the left hand while spooning cereal into his hungry mouth with the right.

I took a sip of water, reminding myself that David used condoms with clients before dropping obediently to my knees. Gently I brought his cock into my mouth, the taste of sweat on my tongue, my lips moving as naturally as the ebb and flow of a tide. As David's dick pulsated and expanded, pleading for release, I feared he'd pull out and ejaculate all over my freshly made-up face – until quite unexpectedly my master's warm cum filled my mouth for the very first time. I took all his juice, used like a submissive semen receptacle, and was rewarded accordingly with his praise.

'You are a very good girl,' David sighed, patting my head as he shook his exhausted dick.

I rose from the floor and spit into the sink (I wasn't that good of a girl), rinsed my mouth then sat down on the couch. David got up to pour himself a cup of coffee. 'I sucked your dick. You at least owe me a cup of coffee.'

'Of course!' David replied, scrambling to pour me a cup. 'Milk and sugar?'

'Just milk.' David handed me my coffee before polishing off another bowl of cereal. 'I still want to do a threesome, you know,' I said slyly.

David laughed in exasperation. 'I know you do! I've been looking for someone for you for six months now! It can't just be anyone. I need a partner, someone I feel comfortable with. You don't want to have bad sex, do you?'

'Isn't there one Latin stripper who –'

'Look!' David interrupted. 'Everyone at the Gaiety either is with their girlfriend, is boring, or is crazy! Most of them are crazy. I'm serious.'

'I believe you. I worked at a dungeon for a year. You don't have to tell me that a lot of people in the sex industry are crazy.'

'How come you never worked as a dominatrix?' David asked, switching subjects.

'Because I hate slaves. I mean, it's all right to hate slaves but not to the point you dread coming into work. That's how bad they annoy me.'

'You'd be good at it,' David suggested.

Was that a comment on my dominantly demanding demeanour regarding a ménage à trois? 'Yeah, I would be,' I conceded. 'I just hate it. I don't like being around submissives like me. All my friends are dominant.'

'I'm like that, too!' David exclaimed. 'I hate being around other tops!'

'So did you have to top your client this morning?' I asked, downing the last drop of java in my mug.

'No, he just wanted to give me a massage and suck my dick a bit.'

'I suck better than your client, right?' I asked worriedly.

'Yes, you suck much better than my client,' David assured, setting his empty cup and bowl in the sink. 'I think I am going to go back to sleep for an hour before I go to the gym.'

I waved goodbye, still glued to the comfy couch. 'I've got to go to work.' Reluctantly I rose and reached for my overnight bag. David escorted me to the door where he picked me up in a big bear hug while I squeezed back as hard as I could. Our lips met in a too-brief kiss.

'I'll see you this weekend, baby,' he said nonchalantly.

And we did see each other that weekend – in a way we'd never seen each other before.

Saturday day came and went without a call from my master. To calm my anxiety I held tight to the knowledge that David had phoned me first thing upon his arrival on Monday. Despite the girlfriend and new boyfriend in his life (or perhaps because of) David still needed his slave. I had to trust that my master's desire for me was as strong as mine was for him. He was just really, really busy. That was all.

Roxanne wasn't up for dancing but I needed to let loose after such an emotional week. Fortunately, my friend Derek was into hitting the city – though he had to catch a bus out of the Port Authority terminal to a friend's beach house at two in the morning. Perfect! We decided to go to the midnight show at the Gaiety (the bus station located mere blocks from the club).

Though David had claimed to be indifferent to my presence at his workplace I decided to phone just to double check. The machine picked up with a different outgoing message. 'Hello. You've reached David and Max. We're at the theatre. If this is an emergency you can get us on our pagers. For David it's –'

Hmm. That's strange, I thought as I jotted down the digits while my master's voice continued with a number for Max. I hung up and tried his pager – which was out of service. I called the apartment once again to leave a message on the machine. As the phone rang I began to relax, realising Max was probably the reason David hadn't called – yet another roommate to get in the way!

'Hi. This is a message for David. It's Lauren. My friend Derek and I are coming to the midnight show tonight. I know you must be really busy so I'll be a very, very good girl and not bother you. We'll probably just sit in the back. If this is a problem call me back before I leave.'

A little over an hour later I was out the door. I arrived a few minutes late and found Derek in front of the 46th Street Howard Johnson's glancing around nervously. 'Derek!' I shouted, waving.

'Oh, good – you're here! I wasn't sure if I was late or not so I went to the theatre and asked if a small brunette girl had gone inside. The owner yelled at me. "No individual girls!"'

'No, I just got here.' I laughed and gave my lanky friend a hug. We ascended the stairs to the seedy strip joint and paid our fifteen bucks each just as the grand finale from the earlier show was getting underway. David was the first dancer to take the stage, cock in hand. 'That's David,' I whispered nervously as we stood discreetly in back by the mirrored wall.

'Which one?' asked Derek as another stripper started to horseplay with my master, throwing his arm around him and simulating butt fucking, making David laugh.

'The first one.'

'Wow! Way to go, Lauren!' Derek cried, impressed. 'He is absolutely gorgeous.'

'I know, I know,' I gloated as the stage filled with erections. Actually, they were all pretty hot – a much better selection to ogle this time, I noted as the final dancer was announced and a chorus of female voices erupted in cheers. Startled, I glanced sideways to find a loud bachelorette party applauding from the last row then quickly turned my attention back to the stage to see who they were applauding for – or rather, what. A stunning black man with a cock the size of a horse's was prowling the runway. What the hell does one do with something that large? I wondered as all the strippers, dicks deflating anxiously, cleared the stage.

As the crowd dispersed I was seized with a sudden strange urge to top my master. Recklessly, I dragged Derek to two second-row seats, wanting David to see me watching him, desiring to be the voyeur and David my sex toy. And I wanted my master to know it. I'd felt so out of control all week. I needed the upper hand – if only for as long as two trance songs.

Derek and I whet our appetites with two beautiful muscle-bound hustlers before David was announced. When the club music came on my master took the runway like a diva, wearing a white net shirt and matching pants. He posed and the crowd cheered – but not loud enough for David. He motioned for them to cheer louder then smiled his smug approval. That was my egotistical master all right – topping the crowd from beneath the bright lights.

As David stalked the runway, treating the audience to his bodybuilder's bulges, he caught my eye with an enigmatic look of acknowledgment before exploding with a demonic energy I thought only I possessed on the dance floor, a warning to match my passion else stay the hell away. David wasn't just dancing. He was *performing*.

David did a cartwheel that landed him directly in front of the group of giggling girls that had now made their way to stage right across from where Derek and I sat as politely as if we were at the Broadway show next door. They screamed for my master like groupies at an arena rock concert –

prompting the disapproving vibe from the usually all-male crowd to grow ever more palpable. I was glad I wasn't the only one wishing these drunken ditzes would pack it up and go home. This wasn't window shopping at Chippendale's, girls – the rest of us were here to buy (or in my case, trade!).

David went backstage to masturbate and reappeared minutes later stroking his ten inches like a peacock shows off his feathers. A roar of applause and dollar bills began to flutter about the stage – even the fucking cheerleading squad was tipping him!

'I'm going to give him a five,' Derek whispered.

'Give him whatever you like,' I shrugged indifferently. 'Just make sure he sees you or else he might give the dance to the guy closest to the stage.'

David spent eternal seconds with all the tippers, displaying his cock like a trophy, shooting his million-dollar grin. He gave a little extra time to the girls (much to my annoyance since they were not paying clients!). As the slow sexy song came to an end my master meandered over to our side, offering the tipper in front of us a close-up of his fat dick while meeting my unblinking eyes. Locked in a battle of the gazes, it was the first time since I'd met David that I didn't back down. On the last note he broke away, leaving the stage. I won. I guess.

'Wow! He is so good,' Derek complimented.

'Do you think he's pissed off that I'm here? I can't tell if he's angry with me or just dominating me with his gaze.'

'I don't know,' Derek answered. 'He did tell you Tuesday night that he didn't care if you came.'

'Yeah, I guess you're right.'

I was still bothered by being unable to read David's face, wondering whether I should have been a good submissive and demurely turned down my eyes for my master, when Front 242's 'Headhunter' blasted from the speakers. Finally, some decent tunes! David had danced to some awful remix of the hippie song 'Horse With No Name'. It was about time I heard something I grew up listening to!

As the industrial beat kicked in the most perfect Latin specimen emerged from behind the black curtain – wearing a cop uniform no less! It was déjà vu from the night I'd met my master, when Jimmy and I had agreed that the 'gum chewer' and the living 'Carlos' doll in the cop uniform that time had been the two hustlers to chat up. 'Holy shit!' I cried, grabbing Derek's hand and pushing him one seat closer to the stage. 'I must fuck him!'

The bronze sculpture prowling the runway removed the tight shirt from his over six-foot frame, revealing a clean-shaven muscular chest. He had a rugged jaw and dark brown hair slicked back to reveal heavy bedroom eyes. He caressed himself slowly and the Girl Scout troop lost their marbles.

While the Adonis went backstage to jerk off Derek threw four singles in my lap. When the Latin stud returned holding a ten-inch cock I made sure to catch his eye before promptly placing two of Derek's ones onto the runway. Nearly everyone was tipping this guy and when he finally got around to us he picked up the dollar bills and smiled at me. 'Thank you,' he mouthed.

I nodded and smiled back coolly, fighting to keep my composure. Then he drifted to the opposite side of the stage to play Chippendale to Britney Spears and company.

Having been blown away first by my master and next by this Latin sensation, it was a good thing the next dancer was a bore. I was wearing my little white submissive PVC skirt and a tight black top with a low neckline – actually the exact outfit I'd worn on my second night with David, the first night we'd played with S&M – and I didn't want to soak the tight skirt. I'd decided against the lucky red dress tonight out of superstition. The red dress had led me to David. Would its power cancel itself out if I used it on the same guy twice? I wasn't taking any chances. Plus, this was a good opportunity to test Roxanne's low neckline theory. She thought it was the cut of the dress and not the dress itself that held the power.

'I want those guys,' Derek suddenly whispered in my ear, motioning to six plain-looking Latin audience members leaning against the wall.

'We're at a strip club filled with beautiful beefcake and you want the customers. I don't get it!' I exclaimed incredulously.

'I like normal-looking people – not this fantasy stuff!' Derek explained.

To each his own, I guess, but personally, I'd take fantasy over reality any day. As I was studying the dirty half dozen along the wall and straining to catch their snippets of Spanish, I couldn't help but notice an ugly old queen hovering a little too close to us. Derek had his bag on the seat beside him and the guy was eyeing it like he wanted to sit there – even though a vacant seat was available right in front of us.

'Oh, I'm sorry. Did you want to sit down?' Derek asked politely once the guy had caught his eye.

'Oh-well-uh-yes, is that one free?' the queen asked anxiously.

Derek removed his bag but I would have none of this sorry excuse for a pick-up. 'Yeah, and so is that one!' I chimed in, pointing directly in front of me.

'You know,' the queen countered, attempting another tactic, 'my friend back there thinks you look very familiar.'

'Which one?' Derek asked, whirling around to look in the general direction the queen was waving at. Sometimes Derek's innocent Mormon upbringing was so apparent.

'The one in the grey shirt.'

'I don't see him. Where is he?'

'Oh, wait! He just left to go to the lounge.'

'Are you buying this?' I finally whispered to Derek. 'This is the lamest pick-up I've ever witnessed.'

'Well, maybe I do actually know the guy,' Derek suggested from the land of Oz.

'From where?' I shot back, exasperated. The queen was still circling vulture-like and it was getting on my nerves. 'Derek, do you want to go back to the lounge and see if you know his friend?' I sighed since getting rid of the prey would also rid me of the predator.

'Yeah, I guess I will.' Derek left with his pathetic escort only to return minutes later. 'Nope, I didn't know him.'

'Surprise, surprise!'

'Oh, wow! I want to tip this one!' Derek exclaimed when he noticed the next dancer, a skinny blond kid with bad posture, ambling down the runway. That figured.

'Oh, gross! He looks like Michael J. Fox on *Family Ties*!' Derek set a couple of bills on the runway as the high school sweethearts screamed with delight. Not only were they obnoxious but indiscriminate as well. It was enough to make a connoisseur of the male form like myself want to throw up. 'I have to pee, Derek, and you have to come to block the door.'

'After this guy,' Derek agreed.

As soon as Alex P. Keaton had finished masturbating I stood up and started walking towards the lounge. Amber's 'Sexual' filled the air, stopping me. 'I love this song!' I cried, singing a few bars to Derek as the next hustler hit the runway. It was the guy who'd simulated butt-fucking my master but I didn't catch his name. 'Yuck! He's ugly, too. I have to pee!'

Derek and I dashed to the bathroom and weren't in line for more than two seconds before the queen swooped down upon us once again.

'Uh-oh, look who's back,' I whispered to Derek as I protectively threw my arms around him. 'Quick – make like we're a couple!'

The queen froze in his tracks as I held Derek close. 'Are – are you two together?' the guy stammered.

'Yeah,' I answered nonchalantly.

'Uh – well, if you're his girlfriend where's his boyfriend?' he joked badly.

'*I'm* his boyfriend!' I shot back, momentarily unbalancing him.

'Um, I won't touch that one,' he said, surrendering with a 'hands off' gesture.

'I didn't ask you to touch it,' I cooed, smoothly delivering the knockout blow.

The queen scampered away in defeat and I marched victoriously into a now empty but still disgusting men's room stall. I applied more bronze to my bitchy mouth before returning to Derek, taking the lead as we sauntered back through the lounge. There was no sign of David but of the three strippers chilling on the riser along the wall one of them caught my lusty eye – the Latin dreamboat. I glanced over my shoulder as I passed him. Yup, he was most definitely staring at me. He smiled so I smiled back.

He rose assuredly and wandered over to where I waited like a shy lamb looking for a hungry wolf.

'I saw you in the audience,' he greeted in a heavy Spanish accent.

No shit – I was the only female tipper who hadn't been screaming like a banshee! 'You were really good,' I said instead. 'I'm Lauren.'

'Fabian. Where are you from?'

'Here. I live in Brooklyn. What about you?'

'Argentina. But I've been here five years. I live in New Jersey.'

'Really?' I laughed. 'Where in Jersey?'

'North Bergen. Twenty minutes from here. I drive in. You come here a lot?'

Now who was getting the bad pick-up lines? But being as how we were in a gay male strip club his query was understandable. 'No, not really. I've been here a few times. I'm with my friend Derek,' I added, motioning to my fag hag who had gotten entangled in yet another fine mess. He was chatting with the queen and his friend.

'You straight?'

'Yeah. Are you?' I asked.

'Uh-huh. I think this will be my last time dancing here. I don't make any money.'

Considering this guy was a walking embodiment of ninety-five percent of the false advertisements in the back of *H/X* magazine I found that hard to believe. 'You don't make any money?' I asked doubtfully. 'Why? Don't you see clients?'

'I do but I won't do anything with them so they don't want me.'

'Oh. Well, I guess you shouldn't be stripping if you're not willing to hustle,' I stated pragmatically. 'What do you do for a living then?'

'I strip.'

'What?'

'For women. I work at a club in Jersey for women. I do bachelorette parties. I also personal train.'

'Oh.'

'But I don't like dancing for only guys. It's different.'

'Well, there are girls here tonight,' I pointed out.

'Yeah, I know. They were loud.' I laughed as Fabian began to warm up to me. 'Come sit and talk with me,' he offered. 'That is, if you want to.'

'Sure.' We sat down on the other side of the lounge and Fabian apologised for his lack of English. 'That's OK. You speak very well. *Yo comprendo un poco de español si quieres hablarme en español.*' As Fabian beamed his killer grin at me I tried to tell him in Spanish that his language was the sexiest in the world. I didn't know how to say 'sexy' in Spanish, though. 'Sexual?' I ventured. Fabian said I could call it 'una lengua sexual' and then, of course, the conversation turned to sex. I congratulated myself on my subject-steering abilities.

'Can we talk about sex?' Fabian asked, his heavy bedroom eyes hypnotising my own.

'Sure, I mean, we are at a strip club.'

'What do you like to do?'

'Well,' I started shyly. 'I guess I like to use my mouth. I'm good with my mouth.'

'Wow! I love that – and I love your eyes,' the Latin wolf added.

'Thanks. They're two different colours.'

'Really?' he asked, moving in for the kill.

'Yup – one hazel, one brown.'

'Ahh, I see that.'

'So what do you like to do?' I inquired, rushing

things right along. 'I love to suck cock. Is that what you like?'

'Oh, yes!' Fabian exclaimed enthusiastically. 'But you know what I would like?' he asked suddenly turning serious.

'What?'

'Well, my fantasy would be for you to – well, this is just a fantasy but –'

'Just tell me!' I blurted impatiently.

'I would like to see you suck one of my friends – and me also.'

'Oh. Well, who is your friend?'

'Andre.'

'Who is Andre?' Fabian nodded to the corner where another stripper had just entered the lounge. The big black stripper. The one with the mutant cock. 'That's your friend?' I said meekly.

'Uh-huh. He's hung like a horse.'

'Yeah, I know,' I sighed. 'Well, when would we do this?'

'Tonight?'

'Uh – don't you guys have clients?'

'I don't. He might. Let me go talk to him.'

As soon as Fabian left to talk to Andre I immediately dragged Derek away from the queens. 'Derek – the Latin stud wants me to go home with him and the big black guy!' I yelled excitedly.

'Lauren, the two queens know David!' Derek shouted back, ignoring what I'd just said.

'So?'

'So they told me David's here tonight with his boyfriend! The stripper who was all over David onstage! That's Max – the guy from the answering machine. That's his boyfriend! Didn't you recognise him from the photo?'

'What?' I was still trying to let all the information I'd just received sink in. 'No. I didn't look that closely at the photo.'

'But David's boyfriend's name is Max! That explains why he's on the answering machine.'

'Well, what the hell is he doing in New York?'

'I don't know,' Derek shrugged sympathetically.

But there was no time to figure out anything since Fabian had returned from his conversation with Andre. Derek left us to talk. 'He doesn't think he has any clients and he says you're cute. It's OK for tonight then?'

'Uh, I guess. Listen – I have to tell you something, though. I know one of the dancers.'

'Which one?'

'David.'

'Oh. You know David?'

'Yeah. He's my master.'

'What?' I tried to explain the concept of a master in English, then in Spanish but finally gave up. 'You have sex with him?' Fabian suggested.

'Uh, yeah. But he's with his boyfriend tonight.'

'Max.'

'Yeah, Max.' My heart sank. Was I the last person in NYC's gay community to find out? 'So I can do what I want. But I want to tell him. I don't have to – *pero yo quiero decir a David para mi. No importa a David. Pero yo quiero decir.*'

'*Bueno.* Tell him then,' Fabian shrugged. 'I'm going outside to smoke a cigarette.'

As luck would have it, the second Fabian left Derek took the seat next to me and David appeared – along with Max. The two hustlers got into a hot and heavy discussion with a client and an eternity passed before David was finally able to break away.

He came over to give me a quick kiss on the cheek then solidly shook Derek's hand. 'I'm David.'

'Derek.'

I gestured for my master to bend down so I could tell him my news. 'You're with your boyfriend tonight –' I started but David interrupted me.

'Yes, I am.'

'No, it's OK. I'm going home with Fabian.'

'You're going home with Fabian?' David repeated with great surprise – and I'm sure a dose of relief that he wasn't going to have to explain himself to me – at least not tonight. 'Fabiano?' he laughed.

'Uh, yeah. Is he OK?'

'Yeah, he's a good guy,' David conceded.

'And he wants to watch me suck Andre.'

'Andre?' David asked as confused as I was. 'Who's Andre?'

'The black guy.' I nodded to the bear of a stripper as he happened to pass by us.

'Him?'

'Yeah. Is he OK?'

'Yeah, he's a good guy, too. They're both good guys. He has a foot-long cock.'

'What?' I asked, losing the words to his French accent.

'He has a foot-long cock.'

'A what?'

'A foot-long cock!' Derek shouted helpfully.

'Yeah, I know,' I said softly.

Just then Max walked over and without even acknowledging either Derek or myself, whispered something in David's ear and stormed away. What an asshole. 'I've got to go,' David said. 'I've got to get ready for my show.' He delivered another quick kiss to my cheek and gripped Derek's hand once again.

'Suck good,' my master ordered as he walked away. 'I'll call you.'

I nodded as he disappeared backstage while the plain new boyfriend, following my master's trail like a lost puppy, shot daggers at Derek and me. Make that an *insecure* asshole that knew, deep down, that hetero-identified bisexual men always chose pussy in the end. No wonder David's girlfriend didn't like the boyfriend. At least she had taste.

'That guy is a total asshole,' Derek observed as Max left the lounge.

'Yeah, well, he knows which side his bread is buttered on. He wouldn't be making any money if it weren't for David. It's obvious they're working as a team. David is sharing his clients with the guy,' I added resignedly. 'Come on. Let's go watch the show.'

Derek and I returned to the theatre just in time to see Andre start his number. He still had his clothes on when a little gay guy came up and tapped me on the shoulder.

'Yeah?'

'Some guy wants you to go back there.'

'What guy?' I asked, squinting towards the lounge.

'Uh, Fabian?'

That's when I noticed the hot hustler peeking out from the doorway, gesturing for me to join him. 'Yes?' I asked uncertainly upon walking over.

'I want to watch him with you but I'm not allowed inside the theatre. You have big cock before?' he pried as Andre returned to the stage, salami in hand.

'Yeah.'

'When?'

'Well, David.'

'David is not big.'

No, David was big. This guy was Guinness Book of World Records. 'He's big enough,' I declared.

'You tell him yet?'

'Yeah, he knows. *Esta bueno.*'

'You are so cute!' Fabian exclaimed, scanning me hungrily from head to toe, the wolf to my Little Red Riding Hood – if Little Red Riding Hood were a slut in PVC.

'Thanks.'

Two minutes later we were joined by one of the goofy white strippers. 'This is my friend Alex,' Fabian introduced.

'Hi. I'm Lauren.'

'Wow! She is so cute!' Alex complimented Fabian.

'Thanks,' I said humbly, 'but there are a lot of cute women here tonight.'

'Yeah, but we like you!' Alex enthused then pinched my cheek like a grandmother. I felt like a piece of fruit.

'You like him?' Fabian asked after Alex left to chat up a potential john.

'No, not at all.'

After Andre had finished slinging his meat there was just one more stripper to go so Fabian left to ready his dick for the grand finale. Derek and I made like wallflowers to watch.

As the dancers took the stage one by one, parading down the runway in their naked fashion show, the night turned ever more surreal. The timepiece had begun melting in the Dali painting that was my mind. My master. His boyfriend. The Latin lover. The black stud. I clapped politely for all. Even Max. He may have been leaving with my master but I was emerging from the Gaiety with my dignity.

* * *

The finale over, Derek and I sat in the lobby with a handful of clients, waiting like anxious groupies for the hustlers to arrive from backstage. 'Lauren!' Derek exclaimed, his voice loud and crystal clear in the emptying club. 'You're the only one left who's not paying!'

'Ssshh,' I pleaded as Fabian exited the dressing room trailed by Andre. Hurriedly, I gave Derek a kiss goodbye, saying I'd call him tomorrow.

When Andre and I were finally formally introduced the first thing I noticed, oddly enough, were his eyelashes. If he were a girl he could have modelled for Maybelline.

'Wow! I think you've got the longest eyelashes I've ever seen on a guy!'

'Thanks,' Andre said self-consciously. 'Where are you from?'

'I live in Brooklyn. What about you?'

'California.'

'I hope northern. I hate L.A.'

'Me, too!' the big bear exclaimed. 'I'm from Berkeley.'

'Well, I guess that's OK then. You work the circuit?'

'No, I just do this on the side. I have a real job.'

'What do you do?'

'Uh, I work with children,' Andre answered mysteriously. Then he let out an embarrassed laugh. 'And that's all I'm gonna tell you.'

'Why? Are you involved in child pornography?'

'No way!' Andre protested, chuckling. 'Exactly the opposite. OK,' he relented. 'I'm a corrections officer.'

'For kids?'

'Yup, juvenile corrections.'

'You like it?'

'I love it.'

'That's good.' Wow – a real live corrections officer. I wondered if he had the uniform with him. 'So you don't have any clients tonight?' I asked as the three of us left the theatre and descended the stairs.

'Nope. But I've got to get up to go fishing with a client at five-thirty in the morning.'

Heading east on 46th Street I glanced back to see David *sans* Max moving in our direction – the wrong way if he was going back to the apartment on 49th Street. How odd – I'd thought he was still inside the club. I pretended not to notice him, though. He was probably meeting a client and besides, I didn't want to flaunt the fact that I was leaving the Gaiety with the two hottest studs with the biggest dicks. I wasn't fucking these guys to spite him. I was fucking these guys to fuck them.

'Did you say fishing?' I asked, turning my attention back to Andre.

'Yeah.'

'Where?' I wondered doubtfully.

'Hell if I know! I'm from California. Where y'all have water around here?'

I laughed. 'You've got to be kidding me! A client is paying you to go fishing? What? In the nude?'

'Nope, I've just got to go fishing with him and his family.'

As Fabian just listened in amazement, I lost all composure, doubling over in a giggle fit. 'Wait a second!' I cried upon finally catching my breath. 'This guy is introducing you to his family? As who?'

'As Andre – I've just got to be my plain old charming self,' he deadpanned.

'Don't you find that a bit weird?'

'Why?'

'I mean, would you go to a strip club, pick up a dancer and take him fishing with your family?'

'Uh, no,' he thoughtfully conceded.

Walking east along 47th Street back to Andre's room the surroundings seemed vaguely familiar and when we stopped in front of the Hampshire Hotel I realised why. Only six weeks before I'd made the mistake of screwing 'Justin' (a Gaiety boy for whom the term 'dumb blond' would have been a compliment) there. A few more strippers and I could have written a Zagat's guide to '*Best Times Square Motels to Fuck a Hustler*'. After Fabian popped into a deli for a bottle of water the three of us took the elevator to the seventh floor.

'You go to the Gaiety a lot?' Andre asked.

'Not really. I know one of the dancers,' I added for the sake of full disclosure.

'Who?'

'David.'

'Who's David?' Andre asked, looking at Fabian.

'The guy with the tattoo on his back – the wings,' he answered in his sexy Spanish accent.

'He's my master,' I stated without further explanation. Being from Berkeley, a stone's throw away from debauched San Francisco, how could he not know about S&M?

'Really?'

'Yeah, but he's with his boyfriend so I can do what I want,' I quickly added. 'He knows what I'm doing tonight,' I said lightly, attempting to radiate easy confidence as we stepped from the elevator and into a brightly lit hallway.

'What's a master?' Fabian asked.

'S&M, man,' Andre answered with a matter-of-fact shrug.

'What?'

'I already tried to explain,' I interrupted. 'It's no use.'

When Andre opened the door to his room I was hit with the all-too-familiar sense of déjà vu. If these cramped quarters weren't where I'd screwed Justin it was damn close – even the general location on the floor was the same. Maybe the Hampshire reserved the room as some sort of 'gigolo special'.

No sooner had I sat down on the bed than Andre began to undress, though not in an overtly sexual way – more like 'this is the first thing I do when I come back from a long hard day of hustling and you just happen to be in the room.' After neatly folding his jeans, he dropped down beside me. 'So what do you like to do?' the big bear asked, lazily stroking his huge appendage.

'Uh, I like to use my mouth. I like to suck cock. Penetration, too, but I don't get off on guys going down on me,' I answered by rote.

'Well, I don't have any condoms so penetration is out.'

My initial disappointment faded as Andre's dick grew longer and wider and more menacing and I realised my eyes were bigger than my pussy. 'You don't use condoms with your clients?' I asked innocently.

'What for? They're not touching my dick.' By now Fabian had undressed and was standing beside the bed playing with his own expanding erection – leaving me the only one left fully clothed without a toy. 'Are you ready, man?' Andre asked the Latin wolf and he nodded solemnly.

'Why don't you show me your skills?' Andre asked, offering me his well lubricated massive black cock. I opened wide as I knelt on the carpet, relishing the challenge, behaving like a porn star in training as I strove to swallow inch after thick inch. Too eagerly I attempted to show off – it seemed as if I was trying to stuff an arm down my throat. 'Use your hand like this. This is how I like it,' Andre guided patiently, his big paw gently enveloping my whole fist, easing it along the wide shaft, my tongue never leaving the wet tip. I felt like I was at a sexual rodeo learning to wrangle the biggest bull. 'That's good. Now you're getting it. You want some of this, Fabian?'

I glanced up to find Fabian nodding enthusiastically so I scooted over to wrap my lips around the more manageable dick. I held tight to Andre's heavy cock (I didn't want to take the chance it would go limp, having been tamed upright into obedience), my hand sliding up and down from head to balls while my mouth and tongue worshipped at the Latin wolf's phallic fountain, praying to be blessed with its warm release.

Soon Andre took the lead once again, suggesting we sample another course on the X-rated menu. 'I want to fuck your face. Come over here,' he ordered nonchalantly. 'Open. Open wide,' he continued in his easygoing tone after he'd manoeuvred me into the proper position – knees to floor, back to bed, head tilted up to touch the hotel mattress built to withstand more than sleep. As Andre thrust his monstrous cock in and out of my mouth instinctively I protected my throat by sucking greedily. 'I said to open your mouth,' he stated calmly.

'I can't deep throat,' I protested meekly.

'I'm not asking you to deep throat. Just open your mouth,' he repeated, his tone both soothing and commanding. As Andre force-fed me his twelve inches he gripped his large shaft in his bear's paw, the head of his dick softly kissing my tonsils. 'You like that, man?' he politely asked Fabian. 'This is good. You want to fuck her mouth?'

The fat black cock between my lips was replaced with Fabian's hard stick of caramel candy. From his ringside seat on the bed Andre cheered on the Latin wolf like an experienced corner man at a bloodless prizefight – the knockout punch to be delivered in a spray of semen. In ultimate submission I let Fabian have his way with my open mouth, his thick dick delivering quick one-two jabs as the voices of the two hustlers floated above me, urgently conversing as if I weren't even there. I felt formed of pliant plastic like a cheap blow-up doll, which made me want to be filled up in every hole.

'You like that? That's good stuff, huh?' Andre whispered. 'Why don't you jerk off all over her face? Fuck her mouth until you're ready to come and then pull out and come all over her face.' Obeying Andre's orders, Fabian shoved his cock in and out until he could hold back no longer. 'Close your eyes and keep your mouth open when he comes,' Andre instructed me.

As warm drops of liquid hit my skin I shut my eyes and licked my lips in anticipation. Usually I wasn't fond of guys coming on my face (well, actually David was the only man who routinely ejaculated on my face) but this time it was different. Being used by two hot guys with Andre's voice echoing like a disembodied porno track made me want to get pounded long and hard like a naughty bitch.

Finally, Fabian's semen spurted fitfully onto my nose and lipstick-smeared mouth, running the length of my neck with his groan of relief. I held mannequin-still, covered in the Latin wolf's warm cum until he returned from the bathroom to tenderly towel every sticky spot on my skin like he was cleaning a spilled meal from a messy child. It was sweet – and so different from my master. David always demanded that I clean myself up – like I was a bad child for being so dirty. Like it was my fault for making him ejaculate. Which made my loins ache with desire as well.

When Fabian returned to the bathroom to rinse himself I hopped onto the bed beside Andre. 'You don't want to come?' I asked surprised as he played lazily with his mighty dick, pouring on Wet, stroking it, sprinkling on more lube – radiating all the enthusiasm of a punk rocker hair-gelling his mohawk into upright submission. Andre seemed intent on getting his cock 'just right.'

'Nope. Play with my nipples.'

'Can I make a phone call?' Fabian asked Andre as I softly twisted the big bear's tits. 'I have a calling card.'

'Sure, just dial nine to get out.'

'So what do you like to do?' I asked Andre as Fabian pushed buttons.

'Everything.'

'But what do you like best?'

Andre paused. 'To please people.'

'Ahh! Now I get it!'

'Get what?' he wondered curiously.

'The reason we're here. You wanted to please Fabian since this is his fantasy.'

'Uh-huh.'

'So I'm not really your type.'

'I don't have a type,' he countered.

'Well, you're treading on my territory if that's what you like to do,' I playfully warned.

'What do you mean?'

'That's what I like to do. I'm submissive,' I explained. 'I like to be used for pleasure. I like to please. Looks like we've got a conflict of interest.'

'Not necessarily,' Andre said mysteriously.

'What do you mean?'

'Turn over – I'll show you. I'll show you what I want to do to you.' Andre manoeuvred my body so I lay face down on the mattress then climbed on top, pressing his hard horse's cock against my short skirt. 'I want to fuck your ass like this,' he whispered in my ear as he brought my head back by the hair. 'Real slow. Then I'm gonna fuck it faster like this.' His massive dick threatened to puncture a hole in my PVC as his bear paw encircled my throat. Then he rolled off of me, leaving both my pussy and ass pleading for more. 'I'll give you my card. I'll be here all week. Call me. I'll do you anytime.'

After numerous attempts Fabian gave up calling his friend. It was time to go – Andre had to be ready to fish with the john in two hours. 'I wish we'd had condoms. I didn't get fucked,' I sighed.

'Maybe we can do this again,' Andre suggested. 'I'm free Monday or Wednesday night.'

'Monday's good,' Fabian said. 'Maybe I bring another girl.'

'Whatever – but I want to fuck her,' Andre concluded, nodding my way.

I smiled, flattered. 'I've got to use your bathroom before we get out of here.'

Andre leapt to his feet. 'I've got to take a piss first,' he proclaimed, beating me to the toilet then left the door open as he stood in front of the bowl. 'Get in here!' he demanded. Confused, I joined him in the tiny white bathroom. 'You're going to hold my dick while I piss.'

Northern California – the S&M capital of the country – his roots were definitely showing, I thought as I grasped Andre's thick cock while he instructed me on properly aiming into the bowl, taught me how to shake the fat head clean. 'Look at this! She doesn't even know how to flush!' he yelled to Fabian while I washed my hands. Apologising, I flushed the toilet with a knowing smile. When we got back to the room he gave both the Latin wolf and me his card. 'Now give me a kiss and get out of here,' the teddy bear ordered.

I gave Andre a childish peck as Fabian opened the door. 'Monday,' Fabian called back as we walked the red-carpeted hallway of the Hampshire Hotel. Once downstairs we took 47th Street to Broadway so Fabian could get his car and I could hail a cab. 'So you like my dick?' Fabian asked shyly.

'*Si. Me gusta mucho. Me gusta mas!*' I answered truthfully. I actually preferred his cock to Andre's for the purpose of penetration. I liked to get fucked, not fisted.

'Monday,' Fabian said as I waved down a cab.

'*El lunes,*' I repeated, receiving his quick kiss before I got inside.

As the yellow cab sped along the Queensboro Bridge back to Brooklyn, my head was spinning with the overwhelming amount of information I'd taken in since Tuesday. I felt like I'd been cramming all week for a college final – and that my role in the events of the evening actually had been my test. I just prayed I'd passed.

Since David wouldn't be back in NYC until November or December it would be a couple months before I knew the score.

The Graduation
(Showdown at the St James Hotel)
(November 2000)

I must have passed September's test since my master couldn't wait to call me when he returned to NYC this time – in fact, he was so anxious that he actually phoned the weekend before he started working.

I was chitchatting with Roxanne, making dance club plans when my call waiting beeped so I clicked over, startled to hear a French-accented hello. Remaining silent, I struggled to wrap my brain around the notion that it was my master's voice since David always arrived on Mondays never Saturdays. 'Is this Lauren?' the voice finally asked.

'Yeah.'

'It's David.'

'You're in town already?' I exclaimed, overjoyed I wasn't dreaming, but David quickly made me wish I were.

'Yeah. I'm with my girlfriend.'

My heart fell to my feet. I had gone from the heights of ecstasy to the depths of devastation in a span of two seconds. A roundhouse kick to the head would have hurt less. 'Oh. Then why are you calling me?'

'We might need an escort for tonight,' my master slowly explained.

'What?'

'An escort,' he repeated. 'I might need a slave this evening.'

'Oh,' I said, my disappointment giving way to mortification. 'You want me to pretend to be a hooker?'

'Yeah.'

'She doesn't know who I am,' I stated softly, beginning to understand.

'She doesn't need to know.'

I took a deep breath. 'But David – I don't like girls. I wouldn't even know what to do with a girl!'

'You'll do what I tell you to do,' my master replied firmly.

And that's when it hit me. David wasn't asking me to pretend to be a hooker for himself and his girlfriend – he was telling me to do it. It was my master's voice ordering me to obey. I had no choice.

'OK,' I heard myself whisper and David mumbled something. 'What?' He answered with a word that sounded like 'nano'. 'What?' I tried again, wondering what the hell he was talking about.

'My girlfriend's name.' I hadn't asked his girl-friend's name – but then I hadn't asked to fuck her either. 'I'll call you in a half hour or so to confirm.'

And then he hung up so I clicked back over. 'Uh, Roxanne?'

'Yeah?'

'Something weird just happened. That was David. You have to help me,' I implored, my voice trembling.

'What? He's in town already?' Roxanne asked, surprised and happy for me.

160

'Yeah. But he's with his girlfriend.'

'What?'

'He brought his girlfriend with him. And he wants me to go over there and pretend to be a hooker.'

'Oh, no,' Roxanne reprimanded. 'No, no, no, no, no! That doesn't sound good!'

'I know it doesn't sound good! But he's my master. You've got to help me figure out what to do!'

'OK. OK,' Roxanne answered calmly. 'Well, I don't think you have enough information yet to make a decision.'

'What do you mean?'

'I mean, what exactly do you have to do?'

'I don't know.'

'Well, you need to find out!'

'Right.' I grabbed a pen and post-it and wrote, *What do I have to do?* 'What else do I need to ask him?'

'Well, what else do you need to know to be a hooker?'

'Um, am I getting paid?'

'Yeah!' Roxanne agreed enthusiastically like I'd just scored the winning answer on *Jeopardy!*

I wrote, *Am I getting paid?* across the post-it. 'What else?'

I brainstormed with Roxanne for a full forty-five minutes before my master called back. 'OK. It's all set. Can you be here in an hour?' David asked.

'Whoa! Wait a minute! An hour? It's only six o'clock. Don't you have to work?' I asked, stunned.

'I'm on vacation.'

'You're on vacation?' I shouted appalled into the receiver before I could bite my tongue. The man who claimed to hate New York was suddenly on vacation here with his girlfriend? This was all too much.

'I start work on Monday.'

'Your girlfriend is in for the week?'

'Just for the weekend.'

A rumble of thunder roiled my insides. With naïve optimism I had thought that maybe David wanted me to play prostitute for the night because it would be the only way to see me with his girlfriend joining him this time. Now I realised that there was no good reason for my master to be calling other than that he wanted a taboo threesome with his girlfriend and his slave.

'Well, what exactly do I have to do? What do I wear? How do I act? I don't know how to be a hooker!' I protested.

'You just knock on the door, I'll let you in, you'll tell me we'll work out the price later –'

'What's the price?'

'You'll tell me it's free.'

'Free? She's going to believe you're getting a free hooker?'

'I'm paying you with my body,' David joked.

I was in no mood for laughter. 'So I'm not getting paid?' I demanded.

'Well, I'll give you a little something if you want. Or I'll get you something new later.'

'Well, what do I wear?'

'Something submissive – very, very submissive.'

'But I don't know how to act like a hooker. How do hookers act?'

'You just come in and I'll tell you exactly what to do.'

'David,' I finally pleaded, desperate for a way out. 'You know this is the most sadistic thing you have ever done to me.'

'Mmm-hmm,' my master answered casually. He was not giving me an exit. The subject at hand was not up for discussion.

'OK, but I need an hour to get ready,' I quietly relented. 'Then it'll take me around forty-five minutes to get there. Where are you anyway?'

'That's fine. We're at the St James Hotel between Sixth and Seventh on 45th. The room is on the eleventh floor – room eleven-four.'

'OK,' I sighed, struggling to stay in the moment to avoid thinking of what I was about to do. As soon as I got off the phone I called Roxanne and let her in on the horrors that lay ahead. 'And I have to be there in less than two hours! I don't even have time to wash my hair or shave my legs!'

'Well, free hooker – what do they expect?' Roxanne replied pragmatically.

Seconds after hanging up, I hurried to the shower then dressed in a frenzy, throwing on a revealing V-neck blouse and purple PVC skirt, yanking a pair of stockings to my thighs against my stubbly skin, dragging my dirty hair into a ponytail – then called a car service.

It wasn't until I was riding over the Queensboro Bridge that I was able to feel. I wondered if David had given me such short notice on purpose – too much time to think and I'd back out. As fury devoured me, I realised that was precisely what he had done. I tried to imagine the night that lay in store, the different scenarios my master might have planned, but it was impossible. I couldn't think. All I could do was feel. And the feeling I had was pure hatred – pure and utter hatred for another human being. I couldn't remember the last time I'd been overwhelmed by such mind-numbing rage. I looked around the interior of the car, ran my hand along the cheap vinyl seat. How much longer before everything around me was consumed by my fire?

The car travelled west on 45th Street down to Sixth Avenue. Spotting the sign for the St James Hotel I told the South American driver to pull over. Then I paid and got out before doing a double-take. Was that really a hotel? Youth hostel was more like it. A far cry from the ivory tower of the Marriott Marquis!

I walked through the lobby that contained nothing but an elderly woman seated behind a plastic shield, and a torn Salvation Army couch. At the ancient elevator I pressed the button and waited. I certainly wasn't going to get any suspicious looks here – at a place surely filled with ten-dollar blow job hos and their bridge-and-tunnel tricks.

After making the rickety ascent with a blond couple speaking an unidentifiable Nordic language I stepped onto the eleventh floor, following the signs until I was able to locate David's room by the '11-4' that was scribbled on the door in blue ballpoint pen. I knocked softly. Maybe no one would answer, I hoped.

'Just a minute,' I heard David call. Moments later the door swung open revealing my master wrapped in a white bathrobe. He ushered me inside.

I didn't look David in the eye but instead walked directly over to where a woman in high heels, stockings, garter belt and black PVC bra lay on her stomach on the bed. She was watching porn on David's DVD player but turned over to stretch out her hand in greeting. 'I'm Lauren,' I said, clasping the small palm as I introduced myself.

'Manon.'

She was definitely a dancer – thin and toned. Yet she wasn't gorgeous. A petite long-haired brunette like myself, without the outfit and make-up she would radiate nothing so much as plain Jane next door. She had a beautiful welcoming smile yet her face seemed older, more worn than I'd expected. I wondered how long she'd been stripping.

'I'm David,' David said, rushing over the minute he'd closed the door. He thrust his hand at me to shake.

'Lauren.'

'This is my wife, Manon.'

Sweetly, I nodded at her in acknowledgment. Wife now? How many more times could he stab me?

'We're looking for a slave tonight,' David continued. 'I want someone who will do whatever I tell her to do. We have sex toys, condoms –' he motioned to where a long, double-headed dildo and several rubbers lay on the nightstand '– and a camera for filming. You can be in the film or just film us, whatever you want to do. If you don't want to do something you just say mercy and we stop.'

I nodded my understanding as I eyed the digital camcorder. Even if I had wanted to respond, David was filling up the silence so fast I wouldn't have been able to get a word in edgewise. Resignedly, I sat down atop the small wooden dresser and leaned back against the monstrous mirror hanging purposefully on the wall.

'What are you wearing?' David asked, coming closer. I removed my light black jacket to reveal the V-neck blouse, keeping my legs crossed as David tugged at the top of my sparkly knee-high boots.

'*Fuck me* boots,' I teased, but in my mind I was screaming, '*Fuck you*, David.'

'Stand up.' I rose tall and proud. With a favourable nod David then glanced back for Manon's appraisal. Catching his eye she mimicked his approval. 'OK. Let's get started. Manon, I want you to sit in this chair over here. Lauren, kneel down between her legs.'

David went into the bathroom to change into his birthday suit, emerging with steel muscles tanned and primed to conquer. 'Lauren, put your hands on her shoulders. Touch her. Manon, you do the same.' As our arms linked she smiled shyly. I smiled back. Then she said something to David in French. 'She wants to know if you're comfortable,' David translated.

'I'm fine.' I grinned reassuringly at Manon. My master was forcing me to fuck his girlfriend who thought I was a hooker. Why wouldn't I be comfortable?

'Good,' David continued, relaxing at the edge of the bed. 'Now kiss her feet.' I knelt down to gently place a kiss on each toe. 'Now her legs. Go up her leg. Use your tongue. Lick it slowly.'

As my tongue tasted the length of Manon's firm leg, she ceased to exist. My master's voice filled my ears and became everything. It was just my master and myself and my focus was not on this strange woman in front of me but on the total obedience that was expected of me. I licked slower and more seductively as David's praises grew louder.

'Very good. Now lick around the pussy. Not on the pussy. Just around it.'

The tip of my tongue circled Manon's stomach, danced over her inner thighs. Was that a pussy behind that black g-string or was I programming the portable DVD player? It didn't matter so long as the instructions came from the man who owned me.

'Good. Manon, stand up. Take off your underwear. Lauren, take off your stockers.' As Manon shimmied out of her g-string I removed my boots and 'stockers'. 'Manon, come over here.' He motioned for his girlfriend to kneel on all fours between his powerful thighs then thrust his cock – my cock – into her open mouth while dominating me with his unwavering gaze. 'Eat her ass,' he commanded as I waited patiently behind her bare butt cheeks.

I sat frozen on my knees, dumbstruck. I hadn't even done that to a guy before! Wasn't there an order to these things? Shouldn't I have at least learned to eat pussy before I ate ass?

David glared menacingly while his girlfriend continued her oblivious cocksucking. Grabbing hold of my hair he dragged me over Manon and into his face. As I tried to look down to avoid my master's eyes he immediately yanked my head back up so I was forced to meet his disapproving stare. 'Do it! Don't make me waste my time!' he said slowly and threateningly.

'Yes, sir,' I whispered. 'Yes sir, yes sir, yes sir,' I continued as David tugged my head from side to side, shaking all thought of free will from my mind before releasing me like a wind-up toy. My lips landed on Manon's hairless crack.

'Now lick it! Not in the hole. Around the hole,' David directed as he leaned over his girlfriend's back to point out precisely where my tongue should go. 'All around here. The inside is for me.' The taste of strawberries filled my mouth as my master's own tongue probed my ear, engulfing it in a passionate kiss. 'You can do better than that!' David barked when I tried to take a break. 'I hope you suck cock better than you eat ass,' he jabbed. 'DON'T WASTE MY TIME!'

Diving between Manon's smooth butt cheeks I tongued like an auditioning porn star. Eating ass was about as exciting as vacuuming my apartment floor but the more David yelled the more I played the role.

I caressed her firm thighs, licked like I was lost inside the asshole of Rocco Siffredi. Something inside took over – and it had nothing to do with obedience. My rebel nature emerged from the slave. A battle call sounded loud and clear in my head. 'Fuck you! You're not going to break me!' Like a little kid laughing in defiance with every lash of the father's belt, I was *not* going to show David any fear. I was *not* going to give him the satisfaction of my crying mercy.

Finally, David arranged a four-legged Manon on the sex-tossed bed with me beneath her on my back, her shaved pussy hovering mere inches from my face. I focused on the little silver balls of her clit piercing as my master's voice boomed omnisciently. 'Lick her pussy – just the piercing. Lick the balls. Suck on them.'

I closed my eyes and stuck out my tongue, transferred my cocksucking rhythm to Manon's clit, playing it safe with what I knew best as my master's fingers roughly rammed inside my dry pussy. I concentrated on their conspiratorial French conversation, which did nothing to dull the pain until I was smacked back to reality by mounds of flesh hitting me in the face. I opened my eyes to find David's balls hanging above as he fucked Manon in her strawberry ass – forcing me to watch from below.

I felt like Alex at the end of *A Clockwork Orange* with nowhere to run from the images of sex thrust upon him as my master and his girlfriend came within moments of each other – both of them roaring like lions, crashing entwined on the bouncing bed. Did all French-Canadians measure ecstasy in decibels? I watched David's bare dick slide from her ass, noted their long-term relationship.

As David made a beeline for the bathroom, Manon turned languidly onto her side. I sat up straight on the bed to intently study the straight porn still playing on the DVD. 'Wow! You are a very good slave. I was not expecting to get such a good slave,' David called, peeking out from the closet-size bathroom.

'It's true!' Manon agreed, nodding at me.

'Thanks,' I answered. Just how good she would never know.

The minute David returned to take a seat on a cheap wooden chair, Manon went to wash up. I could feel my master's gaze hot on my skin but I staunchly refused to meet it, to risk giving access to my thoughts. By the time his clean and carefree girlfriend returned he was no longer seeking it.

They chatted in French as David peeled and ate a banana. They laughed and continued talking together as if I weren't there. 'No English?' I finally asked.

Looking directly at me David replied, 'I like that you can't understand what we're saying.' I nodded and tried to keep the fireball in my stomach from bursting into flame. My master smiled. 'She asked me what I was thinking about and I said "blow jobs".' They laughed again as I stretched out resignedly on the bed. 'You see, we've never done this before,' David continued.

And you'll never do it again, I added in my head.

'So I need to talk to her and see what she wants to do next. If she's comfortable, if she wants to continue with you or alone –'

'No, that's fine,' I interrupted. 'Go ahead and talk in French. I don't mind.' Being excluded from conversation was the minor hangnail of my humiliations that night.

'You want a cigarette?' Manon offered me as she lit one.

'No, thanks. I don't smoke. Don't drink, don't smoke – I'm a good girl,' I smirked.

'Water?' she asked after taking a gulp from the Evian bottle sitting on the nightstand.

'Sure,' I answered and took the bottle from her, hesitating for a moment before putting it to my mouth. Germs, I thought, clearly not thinking straight. I stared at the couple fucking on the DVD, tried to block out the French talk while I swigged Evian.

'OK, we're going to continue alone,' my master finally announced, releasing me. Quickly, I hopped off the bed, dashed to dress. 'Unless you want to stay and film us.' I glanced at the small silver camcorder then back at David and continued to yank my black 'stockers' over my unshaven legs.

'Well, what do you want me to do?' I asked sweet as pie. 'If I'm going to be your slave for the night then you need to tell me what you want me to do.'

Had I lost my mind? I was nearly freed when my pride took over. The 'Fuck you! It doesn't hurt! Hit me harder!' kid had been unleashed and was running straight for the loony bin.

David looked at Manon who shrugged. He shrugged. 'OK. Why don't you film us then?'

After I calmly finished putting on my clothes, Manon showed me how to use the camcorder. 'It's my Christmas present,' she explained happily while gazing through the viewfinder.

I became gripped with nausea. Christmas present. But it was only November. That meant that it had to have been last year's Christmas present at the latest. Which meant that she had been David's girlfriend since at least last year – when he met me. When he told me he didn't have a girlfriend because he was too busy travelling all the time – even though I'd never asked.

To settle my stomach I concentrated on learning the buttons of the camera, which were fairly simple – just a zoom and a record to worry about. Nothing a trained monkey – or a slave – couldn't handle.

As David and Manon took their places on the bed I sat down in what was now my 'director's chair'. Holding the viewfinder to my eye I adjusted for a wide-angle master shot as David rubbed lubricant all over his girlfriend's pussy and ass. I decided that I was now simply the director of my very first porno. It would be all about angles and lighting. I would adjust the camera so it would best flatter my two porn stars. They were two actors and this was my film. There was no David and Manon. No master and his girlfriend. No slave being forced to tortuously watch her master do to someone else what she desperately wanted done to her.

I pressed the record button as David slowly stroked Manon's wet pussy and ass with the double-headed dildo while she gave him an enthusiastic blow job. Her bare butt filled the frame, making it difficult to get a good angle on his dick, so I decided to shoot David's actions instead. As he applied more and more lube I began to grow bored so I zoomed in on her glistening asshole. Then I stood and quickly zoomed back. Then I sat down again. Then I rose to move to the other side of the bed. Then I walked back. Then I leisurely zoomed in on her anxious mouth pumping his hard dick. Then I zoomed back. They seemed to be enjoying each other but I felt numb and restless, their sex play taking forever. The director Bruce LaBruce must have had a hell of a lot of patience.

I returned to the little wooden chair, adjusted for the wide-angle shot. Then I took aim at David's right hand gently fingering Manon's asshole and held steady as I looked up from the viewfinder, searching for something artistic to shoot. My eyes locked with David's. He motioned for me to come closer. Numbness gave way to nausea. He was ruining my movie! If David dominated me then I would feel the pain he was inflicting. As long as I was in the director's chair I was in control. I shook my head in protest.

David's eyes bulged in anger, threatening to pop from their sockets and grab me. With his free hand he once again commanded me to kneel directly in front of him, to position the camera at the foot of the bed.

But the filmmaker in me took over. Fuck you, I thought. How dare you try to play DP when you are a mere actor! I was the one calling the shots! I shook my head even more assertively then stuck out my tongue, daring him to challenge my authority.

In a flash I feared that David would lunge across the bed, snatch the camcorder and smash me with it, such total rage was registered in his gaze. Still I refused to concede. He glared at me for several excruciating seconds before finally backing down. There was nothing he could do. I had the camera – and thus the power to record every feeling he had for me. The slave had topped the master. It was all I could do to hold on to my sanity and keep from throwing up.

David turned his attention back to his cocksucking girlfriend, shoving one of the fat heads of the long dildo into her lubricated ass. Like a wounded animal she cried out so immediately David stopped to gently caress the sore hole. When he tried again she whimpered even louder so he set the dildo aside and held her close, spoke tenderly to her in French. I paused the camera and waited – and witnessed the difference between how David treated his girlfriend and how he treated me. What a wimp she was! I moaned in pain whenever he fucked me – anally or otherwise – but David would never stop or even slow down unless I cried mercy. And even then he'd usually tell me what a bad girl I was for not taking it. If I were in the movie the camera would still be rolling. DON'T MAKE ME WASTE MY TIME!

I waited, slumped uncomfortably in the chair, until David began to fuck her doggy style. Pressing the record button, I wandered over to the dresser where I sat down, pointing the camera at the monstrous mirror for a reverse angle shot – an artistic flourish! As David thrust his big cock in and out of her recovered asshole, I aimed directly at their quivering bodies. Manon fingered her pierced clit fast, moaned in ecstasy, came with a call of the wild, collapsed onto the bed. Quickly, David pulled out so she instantly flipped onto her back, mouth open wide. She knew the drill.

David jerked off until he had covered her face in his wads of cum, roaring like he was auditioning for the Discovery Channel, then fell forward, landing on top of her. Their laughter mingled in their tangled heap. Quietly, I turned off the camera and returned it to its place on top of the nightstand.

When Manon left for the bathroom David looked over to where I waited silently by the dresser. 'You ready to go? You have all your things?'

'Uh-huh.'

'OK.' David threw on his bathrobe as Manon returned and thanked me for coming.

'You're on vacation?' I asked her.

'Yes.'

'Well, enjoy.'

David grabbed a roll of hundreds from a drawer and escorted me to the door. He pretended to hand me a few bills and I faked taking them. Then I searched his eyes for something to say.

Without a word David kissed me on the cheek and opened the door.

Once I stepped outside and into the midtown chaos of 45th Street I started to shake. I felt sick and disoriented, like a car crash victim who doesn't feel the pain until reaching the safety of a hospital. I walked unsteadily to a phone booth, anger and humiliation filling my every pore. I called Roxanne but she wasn't home so I tried Derek on his cell. 'Derek! I'm so glad I've gotten in touch with you!' I exclaimed jubilantly when he answered on the third ring.

'Hey!' he enthused then paused. 'Who is this?'

'It's Lauren,' I replied, my voice trembling.

'Lauren?' he said surprised. 'You don't sound OK. Are you OK?'

'No, I'm not,' I sighed. 'Where are you?'

'Um, I'm walking down 49th and Eighth right now.'

'Oh, wow! I'm on 45th and Sixth. I'm on the corner. Can you come get me?' I pleaded.

'Of course. I'll be right over.'

Ten minutes later I spotted Derek. When he greeted me with a loving hug all the walls I'd been building up inside came crashing down. 'Derek, you're not gonna believe what happened to me. David's in town.'

'Already?'

'Yeah, I just saw him. I have to tell you what just happened but you can't make any judgments, OK?' I said in one breath.

'OK,' Derek agreed, wrapping his arm around my shoulder, bringing my shivering body into the warmth of his leather jacket. Silently, I said a prayer of thanks to the guardian angel responsible for delivering my fag hag to me on this bitter evening.

The wind fought against us as we walked west. As I spun my tale, the fireball that had been sitting in my stomach all evening suddenly exploded onto Derek. I was practically running down the street, whirling like a dervish – just the latest crazed Times Square attraction.

'Here,' Derek offered, holding up his backpack like a shield after an arm had swung within inches of his poor pretty face. 'Do you want to hit this?'

'No, I don't want to hit anything,' I exhaled, exhausted. 'I don't even want to feel anything. Can we just go to a diner or something? Roxanne should be home pretty soon and we have plans to go dancing tonight. Maybe we could get coffee by her apartment and I'll call her when we're through.'

Derek and I found a Greek diner on 43rd and Ninth. After we'd ordered our coffee I apologised for ruining Derek's plans for the evening.

'No, it's OK,' he protested earnestly. 'Just tell me what I can do for you. What do you need?'

'I need cock,' I answered honestly. I'd certainly eaten enough pussy to fill me for the rest of my life.

'OK. What do you want to do?'

A light bulb popped up between my loins. 'Can we go to the Gaiety? I really need to see big hard dicks. I've been eating pussy all night.'

'Hmmm,' Derek mulled. 'When's the next show?'

The kitchen clock on the wall above the counter read quarter past ten. 'Well, we can still make the ten-thirty.'

'OK,' Derek willingly replied. 'Let's get the check.'

Derek paid the bill while I went to the bathroom to reapply bronze lipstick and straighten out my ponytail and my overloaded head. I tried Roxanne on Derek's cell but she still wasn't home so we headed back over to 46th Street, Derek's arm around me attempting to soothe my frazzled nerves. 'You know, you remind me of Buzz in *Rebel Without A Cause*,' my fag hag mused. 'When they're doing the car races and he goes off the cliff. You're the type of person who doesn't know when to jump. You'd rather go over the cliff.'

'I think you're right,' I conceded.

When we arrived at the Gaiety, Derek had to pay my way in since I'd spent nearly all my cash on the car service getting to David's hotel then had forgotten to ask for reimbursement. After financing my own humiliation I was left with only a five-dollar bill and my stubborn pride.

It was impossible to find an empty seat in the jam-packed theatre so Derek and I stood by the wall as a very buff hustler prowled the runway. Shocked more by the size of the audience than the length of the guy's dick, I asked my favourite security guard if the ten-thirty show had started already.

'Nine-thirty show. It starts at nine-thirty on the weekends,' the bouncer who reminded me of Santa Claus (if Santa Claus were a Buddhist from Sri Lanka) explained.

Finally, a couple of seats near the stage opened up so Derek took one and I collapsed into the other just

as a sultry caramel-coloured specimen hit the floor.
'He's hot but he's too pretty,' I opined dismissively.
'Not my type.' After removing his shirt to better
caress his shaved chest, the dancer flexed his biceps
self-assuredly. 'Hmmm. I like his attitude, though. I
like how he owns the dance floor,' I continued in my
critical analysis while the guy went backstage to get
his erection. Minutes later he emerged from behind
the heavy black curtain, a fat ten inches in hand.
'Hmmm. Maybe he is my type,' I concluded.

Short on tip money, we simply watched as the
crowd showered the stage with its approval. A small
grey-haired man in the front row, unable to contain
his enthusiasm, kept leaping up out of his seat,
clapping wildly as if witnessing one of the Tony-
nominated performances down the block. It was the
first time I had ever seen a standing ovation given at
a strip club. It was the first time all night I had
laughed.

The brunette beauty scooped up his greenery,
making a quick exit before a bleach blond took the
stage. 'Ooh, he's hot!' Derek declared as the muscular
stripper with the white crew cut strutted his stuff.

'A blond! Yuck!' I sighed.

But as the dancer slid out of his sweater, stalking
the runway in nothing but bulge-highlighting blue
jeans, my pussy voted with Derek. His soft feminine
face left plenty to be desired but that body was
fucking ideal – with matching arrogance to boot. All
he needed was the hard hat to be the perfect
construction worker fantasy. He could drill me any
day.

The stripper disappeared behind the heavy black
curtain, emerging with his precious moneymaker in
hand. Derek gave me two dollars to lure him with

but, alas, he never offered us a dance. I decided to use the perpetually grimy men's bathroom before the next stripper's show then called Roxanne from the lounge while simultaneously cruising for meat on my way back. There were a couple of Latin strippers hanging out by the videogame, neither of whom piqued my interest, and two old queens consuming punch and pretzels by the complimentary refreshment stand. The room was exceptionally quiet, with the air of a sad high school reunion. When Roxanne picked up the phone on the third ring I immediately launched into a tirade about David.

'Lauren! Wait! Where are you calling from? I hear music in the background.'

'I'm at the Gaiety!'

'What are you doing at the Gaiety?'

As I related the events that led to my pathetically ending up in a gay strip club the lounge began to fill with dancers. The bleach blond construction worker drifted towards me as if from the cover of a Harlequin Romance – then, seeing the cell phone glued to my ear, abruptly stopped and turned to converse with one of the paying patrons. 'Oh, shit! I just lost one!' I yelled into Derek's mobile.

Strippers strolled by in an unsubtle manner, flashing smiles like they were auditioning for my casting couch. Which I guess they were. When I noticed the caramel dream staring directly at me I decided it was time to hang up. 'Look, Roxanne, I've got to go. I'm being cruised by strippers. I'll call you after the show. We can figure out what we want to do then. Bye.'

'Hi, I'm Ronnie,' the hustler said the minute I'd unstuck the phone from my ear.

'Lauren.'

'You're from here?'

178

'Yeah, I live in Brooklyn,' I answered casually. 'What about you?'

'Houston.'

'You're from Texas?' I asked disappointed. Another American. Sigh.

'Yeah.'

'Well, I actually grew up in Colorado,' I admitted.

'What are you doing here?'

'I'm a writer and a filmmaker.'

'No, I mean here. You come to this club a lot?' he clarified with a hint of southern twang.

'No, I'm here with my friend Derek. He's gay,' I explained, happy to have a homosexual around as an excuse for my X-rated indulgences.

'Oh. I saw you in the audience. I was wondering what you were doing here. What are you doing after the show?' he added smoothly.

'I haven't decided yet,' I answered indifferently. 'I might go dancing. What are you doing?'

'I'm supposed to go to a club called Exit.'

'I've never been there. Who are you going with?'

'A couple of other strippers – my roommate and maybe another guy.'

'Oh, well, I can't really make any decisions about where I'm going until I ask my friend Roxanne. We're supposed to go out later. I'm going to call her after the show.'

'Let me give you my number,' Ronnie suggested. 'You can call me on my cell phone if you want to meet up with us. We won't be getting out of here until around three in the morning.'

'OK,' I agreed. 'Do you have a card?'

'Uh, no. Do you have a pen?'

'No.'

'Wait right here. I'll be right back.'

As soon as Ronnie dashed off I phoned Roxanne again. 'Hey! Do you want to go to Exit with some strippers tonight?'

'Oh, wow!' she cried excitedly. 'Are they paying?'

'I'm sure they will.' I knew a free club night would get the dancing queen all hot and bothered. 'I don't have any money anyway. But we won't actually be going until three in the morning,' I warned. 'They don't get out of work until then. We'll have to kill a couple of hours. Do you still want to do it?'

'Hmmm –'

'You know what?' I interrupted. 'I should just come over there after the show and we can see how we feel. I've got the guy's cell phone number. If we want to go then I'll call him.'

'OK, that sounds good,' she agreed.

'I'll be over around midnight. Bye.'

Moments after I hung up Derek appeared, a bored look in his eye. 'Are you ready to leave pretty soon?'

'Oh, yeah, sure. Do you want to walk me over to Roxanne's? Can I borrow twenty bucks?' I wondered, figuring five wasn't enough to eventually get me home.

'Sure,' he yawned.

On our way out I told Ronnie I'd call him if we decided to go. Then it was back to 43rd Street yet again.

Arriving at Roxanne's I thanked Derek for saving my sanity before wishing him safe journey back to my Bleecker Street apartment he was subletting. Alone with the Russian diva and her Pomeranian, Pokey, I launched into another tirade about David, explaining in graphic detail the psychological torture I'd suffered at the hands of my cruel master.

'Stop! Stop! I don't want to hear any more!' Roxanne pleaded. 'I'm getting jealous!'

'What?' I exclaimed, shocked.

'Of her! I want a boyfriend who will hire a hooker to go down on me,' Roxanne sighed dreamily.

'I've just been through the most sexually traumatic night of my life and you're jealous of David's girlfriend?' I asked, appalled.

'Yeah.'

'Well, I was a damn good slave,' I bragged ruefully. 'I could tell she was impressed.'

'Now she'll be expecting the same treatment from all the other hookers they get. You've ruined it for her. David will have to say, "Honey, it can never be as good as the first time."'

By the time Roxanne had put together her pink outfit and I'd shed the red angst from my system it was two in the morning. I dialled Ronnie an hour later. He and his roommate were just leaving the theatre so I suggested they stop by to pick us up since we were only five blocks away. After inexplicably getting lost and phoning back for directions, the Texas longhorns finally found their way to Roxanne's walkup where we were introduced to Gregory, a short plain-looking black guy whose strip show I'd fortunately missed. He stared wide-eyed at Roxanne's pink themed studio complete with bunk beds and vintage new wave posters on the wall. Barbie meets Gary Numan. 'I know,' I offered with a sigh. 'It's like an alien spaceship in here.'

The temperature had dropped about twenty degrees since I'd left my apartment eight hours earlier so I borrowed a faux leopard-fur jacket while Roxanne wrapped herself in her pink-polka dot coat. Thus properly dressed in party attire the four of us set out for Exit.

Since there was only room for three in the back seat of the taxi, Ronnie set me on his lap, his strong arm encircling my waist like a warm seat belt while Roxanne was pinned between the two testosterone-heavy bodies. 'I just want everyone to know that I am an asexual being,' she announced out of the blue, causing a brief awkward silence.

'What?' the two dancers asked simultaneously, confused.

'She just wants everyone to know that she doesn't do sex,' I translated.

The two strippers looked at each other and shrugged as the cab stopped abruptly at the club. Though it was close to four in the morning Exit stayed open until eight so the line to get in was still quite long. Taking our place at the back we surveyed the crowd – a pure bridge-and-tunnel nightmare. Drunken Phi Beta boys were falling over the velvet rope as Jersey girls screamed like cats at one another. As a limo slowly drove by a Guido girl ran after it, threw open the backseat door and started bitch slapping the woman inside. It was like a cattle call audition for the latest reality TV series.

'Are you sure you want to go here?' I hesitantly asked Ronnie.

'I guess,' he shrugged as another fight broke out right in front of us. 'Uh, maybe not.'

Foregoing Exit we drifted down Eleventh Avenue in search of some diner that Roxanne liked. Ronnie put his arm around me and we coupled off to get down to business. 'You can come home with me,' I offered waveringly. 'But I live in Brooklyn with my sister.'

'Well, you can come back with me if that's easier.'

'What about your roommate?'

'He doesn't care.'

'Really? Where are you staying?' I inquired, the deal nearly sealed.

'The St James Hotel,' Ronnie replied as we reached a big roadside diner misplaced in midtown Manhattan. Having been fucked by fate I was still trying to retrieve my libido from the pavement when Roxanne noticed a nightclub attached.

'Let's go inside!' she exclaimed, recognising the tune booming from the entrance.

'Can't we get some food first?' I snapped. David had given me barely enough time to dress let alone eat dinner and low blood sugar was making the night even more surreal.

The four of us entered the diner and ordered breakfast. While Roxanne and Gregory bonded over the odd coincidence that they were born on the exact same day of the exact same year ('long-lost Gemini twins' according to Roxanne) I poured my aching heart out to Ronnie, who listened dumbstruck as I described my lesbian humiliation at the hands of another hustler.

'So your roommate doesn't care if I come back with you guys?' I double-checked.

'No.'

'What? Does he want to watch?'

'If you want him to.'

'He wants to join in?' I continued, the void inside filling with debauched possibilities.

'If you want him to,' Ronnie repeated in his carefree tone.

'You guys have done that before?' I asked, surprised.

'Yeah, we're roommates back in Texas. We've lived together for over a year.'

Two threesomes in one night? That would definitely be a record for me, I thought, buttering my bagel and ignoring Roxanne who had been vying for my attention for the last ten minutes intent on going dancing next door. Fed up, she suddenly stormed out. Shocked into regret, I jumped up and ran after her, chased her down the street like a guilty lover, begging forgiveness. Unmoved, she refused to return so I went back and borrowed Ronnie's cell, calling her at home once we'd paid the bill and left to hail a cab.

Thank goodness I'd made up with Roxanne by the time we reached the St James Hotel since I didn't need the fury of a friend hanging over my head along with my master and his girlfriend who slept four floors above where my second ménage à trois of the night was about to take place. Fortunately, Ronnie and Gregory were bunking in a renovated part of the St James, which lacked the thrift store furniture smell and I breathed a sigh of relief once I was safely locked behind their closed door.

I lay back on the bed and watched the two strippers undress, content to be invisible for the moment. Naked, his dark muscles glistening, Ronnie stretched out beside me and held me gently in his arms. Our tongues finally met for the very first time. Softly I teased the stud's hard nipples as he tugged off my low-cut blouse, slipped my PVC skirt from my waist. His hands continued their treasure hunt under my Victoria's Secret bra and my black thong while Gregory kept his ear to the wall, listening to the crazy lady next door talk way too loudly to her television set. His laughter was distracting me.

'If you'd rather listen to her than play with us, go right ahead. I wouldn't want to bore you,' I said cattily.

Gregory glanced over to find Ronnie nibbling on my right tit while fingering my pussy. 'Look! It's shaved!' Ronnie enthused to his roommate like he'd discovered lost gold.

'Oh, wow!' Gregory answered excitedly.

'So? You must sleep with a lot of strippers with shaved pussies,' I ventured as Ronnie continued to explore the delicate skin.

'Not really,' he answered innocently as his roommate joined us. Gregory catered to my left half, his tongue sampling my hard nipple, his hand exploring my bare pussy while Ronnie mirror-imaged every movement on the right. I relaxed, melting into the role of star attraction that I'd been seeking all night. I wasn't a free hooker, a sex toy to be tossed aside post-orgasm. I was something special.

I wrapped my lips around Ronnie's stiff dick, rinsing Manon's strawberry taste from my mind with pre-cum, then rolled Gregory's erection luxuriously around my tongue like a cock connoisseur at a tasting party. When Gregory put on a condom so he could fuck me doggy style Ronnie gladly took back my magic mouth, drilled deep with desire. I lost myself in cock. Cock, cock, cock. When I told Derek I needed cock I had no idea I'd be granted this much!

Suddenly Gregory's dick slid from my pussy, forcing its way inside my non-lubricated ass with a single thrust. Too exhausted from the endless night to fight I relaxed and rode the bucking hard-on as best I could. 'Oh, shit!' I cried as he dove further down the hole. 'He's fucking my ass,' I whispered to Ronnie.

'Oh, yeah!' Ronnie exclaimed, overjoyed as he grabbed a rubber. 'Wait! Let me move down.'

Seconds later I found myself straddling the stripper then felt his pumping dick plunge into my soaked pussy. As both holes filled with expanding flesh I was fucked into a state of euphoria, amazed at how wonderfully whole and complete the world seemed. I stared into the jumbo mirror on the wall – identical to the one in David's room four flights up – and watched as two hot porn stars performed double penetration on a triple-X starlet. Moaning, groaning in ecstasy, their bodies moving in synchronicity, they morphed into a single entity. I wanted to call David and have him come down with the camcorder.

Gregory exploded inside my ass, removed his spent cock just as Ronnie lost his precious juice inside my pussy with a grunt of relief. His polite dick stayed hard until my own orgasm bubbled up, erupting with a force that caused my limp body to spill on top of him. We all collapsed exhausted into the molten mattress for several minutes – then they both wanted blow jobs.

As I opened wide for Gregory's insatiable organ, Ronnie begged to fuck my ass. I told him that it would have to wait – I'd met my anal penetration quota for the evening – so instead we made tentative plans to see each other again the following weekend. 'David's still in town, though,' I added hesitantly, 'and I need to see him as well. Maybe we could all have sex together. Kill two birds with –' I stopped myself when I realised how horrible that sounded.

Ronnie laughed. 'No, that's OK. I understand. Uh, is David into guys?' he continued warily.

'Well, he's bisexual. But don't worry,' I assured. 'You are definitely not his type. What are you anyway? Your background, I mean.'

'African-American and Cherokee.'

'Oh, that's interesting. I thought you were Latin. What about him?' I asked, pointing to Gregory who, blow job interrupted, had fallen asleep at the foot of the bed. 'I mean, does he want to do an orgy?'

'I don't know. Ask him.'

'Hey, Gregory!' I yelled, startling the stripper awake. 'You want to do an orgy with David?'

'Who's David?'

'Another stripper that I see.'

'He's straight?'

'Bisexual – but you're not his type.'

Gregory made a face. 'Bisexual? No! Yuck!'

I became infuriated – how dare a gay-for-pay hustler make a judgment on someone else's sexuality! 'Well, you just fucked a gay boy in a woman's body! What does that make you?' I spat.

'What?' Gregory asked confused, then shook his head and returned to his dreams. Ronnie just waved him off like a long-suffering wife.

It was seven in the morning when I left the St James Hotel for the final time, twelve hours after I'd begun my strange odyssey. Ronnie called a car service then escorted me down to the lobby at my request since I was still paranoid I'd run into my master. It wasn't until I'd stepped past the transvestite hooker sleeping on the couch and the elderly woman counting the night's receipts behind the plastic shield that I let out a sigh of relief. I gave Ronnie a brief kiss but refused to let him pay for my carfare – he'd done enough already by saving my sanity. Then I melted into the vinyl seat of the livery cab, happy that I was too exhausted to feel.

I didn't hear from my master again until the following Thursday afternoon when I called my machine to check my messages before leaving work. My heart skipped a beat when I heard his voice, formal and businesslike, sounding about as friendly as a bored telemarketer telling me to phone on his cell. So I immediately called Jimmy.

'Help – David's on my answering machine at home! He sounds really serious. If he dumps me after what he put me through on Saturday I swear I'm going to have to be committed to an asylum!' I cried breathlessly.

'If he dumps you then you won't have to deal with all this craziness anymore,' Jimmy sanely replied.

'Wow! You're right. I never thought of it that way. I guess that's why I called you. I need to hear from a rational head.'

'Just wait until you get home to call him,' he warned. 'You don't need to deal with this at work. You know, you may just be misinterpreting his voice. After all, you two really didn't talk after what happened. He's probably not sure how you feel about all this. He might just be on the defensive.'

'Yeah, I guess you're right. I could just as easily dump *him* over this,' I realised, so I thanked Jimmy for his advice, took a deep breath and headed home.

I was fairly calm until I got back to Brooklyn, when a swarm of butterflies invaded my stomach a block away from home. I wished that life could be simple again. I wanted fun and games without consequences. Steadying my soul, I bounded up the steps to my front door and up the second flight to my apartment, then once inside made a beeline for the phone before the butterflies could devour me whole. As soon as my hand touched the receiver it rang. Startled, I picked up. 'Hello?'

'Hi. It's Michael,' came the creepy voice from the other end, causing my weirdo radar from my managing days at the dungeon to kick in.

'You must have the wrong number,' I said firmly. 'I don't know anyone named Michael.'

'Uh, no, I don't. Don't you remember you met me – uh – in front of – uh – the school?'

Oh, yeah – that's right – the school I don't go to.

'Nope, sorry.' As I hung up and tried to dial David it rang again.

'Hi. It's Michael.'

'Look, I don't know anyone named Michael!' I shouted, starting to lose it.

'Just give me one minute to –'

'No! Get off my phone!'

When I hung up it only rang again so I decided to let him talk to the answering machine but by now Jordana, who had been listening to me wrangle the pervert, wanted in on the action. 'STOP CALLING THIS NUMBER!' my sister screamed into the receiver that she'd grabbed from my hand before smashing it back in its cradle.

The phone rang again so she picked it up and screamed the same thing, slammed the receiver down so it could ring again. 'Let the machine pick up!' I snapped at her.

'No! Then he'll leave a message!'

'He's not going to leave a fucking message! He wants to talk to a live girl. That's the point. He just wants to hear a woman's voice. If he hears the machine then he'll stop calling back. Trust me! I was a receptionist at a fucking dungeon for a year! I know how to deal with phone freaks!' I yelled like a nutcase.

The machine picked up – and we got rid of Michael. I calmly phoned David.

'Hello?' answered the French accent after the second ring.

'Hey, David. It's Lauren,' I said, trying to make my voice sound light.

'Hey. What are you doing?'

'I just got home from work. What are you doing?'

'Eating. I'm at a restaurant.' A busy one, I

discerned, from the racket going on in the background. 'What are you doing tonight?'

'I haven't figured it out yet. My friend Aimee is supposed to fly in from Iceland this evening. She had originally wanted to go to the Gaiety but she thinks she'll be too tired so we'll probably just hang out and have coffee. Why?' I wondered rhetorically.

'I was thinking about using you tonight.'

'Well, what time?'

'Midnight or twelve-thirty.'

'I could probably do that,' I relented, all my defences down. 'I'm not sure where I'll be at midnight, though. I could always check in with my messages –'

'Well, I'll call you before to confirm.'

'OK. You know you owe me a big reward, though,' I added.

'No. You owe me.'

'What?' I asked baffled. 'Why?'

'I can barely hear you in this restaurant!' David complained. 'Why do I owe you?'

'Because I was a very, very good girl on Saturday.'

'No, you weren't.'

'Yes, I was!' I exclaimed decisively.

'You didn't give my girlfriend an orgasm,' my master nonchalantly countered as he chewed, shocking me speechless. 'So you can bring a whip tonight?' he continued.

'I told you before – I don't have a whip!' I reminded, regaining my voice.

'OK, just bring rope then. I need about ten feet of rope.'

'David!' I protested. 'I don't have any rope either. Where am I –'

'Just do it!' my master barked.

'Yes, sir,' I sighed.

'I'll call you in a few hours.'

'OK.' After hanging up I phoned Derek at his short films on the Internet job so he could listen to me complain while he readied to leave the office. 'I don't believe this! And on top of everything I need to find ten feet of rope!' I cried.

'Hey, we just had some sort of S&M shoot here last week! Maybe they left some rope. Dion, do we have about ten feet of rope lying around somewhere?' Derek helpfully asked his co-worker. 'No? No, we don't. Sorry.'

'That's OK. I'll figure something out,' I said before thanking Derek for his ear. Then I decided to take a long hot bath while I awaited Aimee's call. When she still hadn't phoned by ten I correctly assumed that between the jet lag and five-hour time difference she'd probably fallen asleep. At half past my master called to let me know we were on for twelve-thirty.

'I couldn't find any rope, David. I tried but the store didn't have any nylon and the other kind will give me burns,' I lied.

'OK, just make sure you wear something very submissive,' he ordered. 'No bra and no underwear.'

'Yes, sir. Anything else?' I asked sweetly.

'Hmmm.' David paused to ponder the question. 'Glasses.'

'Glasses?' I repeated, recalling the bleach blond construction worker fantasy from Saturday and how sexy he'd looked in his granny glasses. I didn't have any granny glasses. 'My regular glasses or sunglasses?'

'Bring both. You have your period?'

'Uh, yeah, I'm at the end of it. Why?'

'Just curious.'

'Oh. So should I call you before I come over?'

'No, just be here at twelve-thirty,' my master commanded before hanging up.

I slipped into a snug-fitting leather corset, tight miniskirt that outlined my ass, attached a black lace garter belt to the 'bitch' stockings David had bought for me back in April. I dragged my knee-high 'fuck me' boots up over my muscular calves then combed out my freshly washed hair. I was a shining example of whorish white trash, slave collar round my neck like a cherry on top. My master would be pleased.

Since it was raining I phoned for a car at eleven-thirty, figuring I'd have to wait a while for a driver to be dispatched, but the livery cab arrived five minutes later. Sailing smoothly along the slick city streets, I was overcome by the beauty of Manhattan at midnight when unsophisticated star-struck tourists give way to its jaded moonstruck residents. How different I felt journeying into the city this time around! On Saturday I'd been shocked by the hate burning inside but now I was equally stunned by the utter serenity of my soul. Having given up fighting, abandoned myself to the loss of control, I was wholly calm! Since meeting David not once had I ever approached an S&M tryst with such a sense of peace. Was this what 'happiness in slavery' truly meant?

I'd always preferred to be the passenger in the car, even fought my mom long and hard against getting my driver's licence when most teenagers couldn't wait to slide behind the wheel. I loathed the responsibility, wanted only to relax and enjoy the view. David was more than willing to act as my chauffeur on this S&M journey. I'd given him the keys to my life – and in so doing, relinquished the heavy responsibility. Feeling privileged to be seated by his side, I was resigned as well to the certainty that I would be kicked out of the car the minute I started giving directions. I needed David to drive me to the place where I'd discover myself. Besides, I'd let my licence lapse years ago.

I rang David's buzzer at exactly half past twelve. Receiving no reply I turned to open my umbrella back up when I noticed the lone figure in black leather pants swaggering confidently down the street. When my master reached the bottom of the stoop he stopped to stare up at me with the eye of an art critic admiring a statue on a pedestal. He nodded his approval.

'You look good,' David declared.

I said nothing but coyly opened the bottom of my long leather coat so he could read the bitch stockings. David nodded again then bounded up to meet me and unlock the front door.

I felt like a dog returning home as I skipped ahead of my master, obediently ran upstairs. David pushed open the apartment door for me and I walked through the brightly lit hallway to wait mutely by the couch while my master loaded soda into the fridge. Next he unwrapped his present by taking off my coat. Though his eyes grew wide upon seeing the leather corset and miniskirt David showed no other signs of being impressed, simply motioned for me to take a seat on the couch while he removed his own jacket. I dropped onto a soft cushion and crossed my 'fuck me' boots defiantly.

'Hey! Why are you wearing underwear?' David reprimanded, observing my body from across the room.

'I have my period.'

'Oh.' He grabbed a diet Coke from the refrigerator. 'You want Coke? Water?'

'Water, please,' I answered as my master popped a hardcore movie into the VCR. 'Have any gay porno?' I inquired.

'No.'

'Wrestling?' I tried.

'Wrestling?'

'Yeah, wrestling turns me on. The Rock!'

'No, but you'll like this one,' David assured as Latin tits and cocks filled the screen. 'It has guys in it.'

'That doesn't make it gay porno,' I complained as my master returned to the kitchen to pour me a glass of water.

'So how was it?'

'What?'

'Saturday.'

'What do you think?' I retorted cattily.

David turned to look directly at me. 'I'm asking you a question.'

'I hated it.'

'Good. It's good for you to do things you hate.'

'Is that why you vacation in New York? Because you hate New York?'

David smiled. 'I don't hate New York. I don't really know New York. But, yes, it's good for me to do things I hate. So, what did you hate? The taste, texture?'

'Everything. It's not that I hate girls. I just don't like them.'

David took my glass of water and his soda over to the small table and sat down. He spread his legs widely, motioned me between them. 'Over here. I need a foot massage. Take off my shoes,' he ordered, extricating rolling papers from a bag.

I knelt on the hardwood floor between my master's legs as he rolled a joint, unbuckled one shoe then the other. Even his militaristically shined shoes were sexy! The soft leather and gleaming buckles stirred my pussy as much as his bulge-enhancing leather pants. When he removed his black shirt to reveal his perfectly sculpted abs I longed to trace each muscle with my tongue.

'Way!' David praised when I tugged off the sweaty socks. 'Now take off my pants.' I jerked my master's pants from his legs, draped them neatly over a chair then obediently fell to the floor to work on his sore soles. 'So that's the first time you've been with a girl?'

'Yes.'

'Good. Now you'll have to get me one of your girlfriends,' he continued matter-of-factly.

I dropped his foot in a fit of laughter. 'David!'

'What?' he asked while lighting a joint.

'None of my friends would .put up with you!' I shouted, bursting into more giggles.

'What do you mean?' he asked, bewildered.

'I mean all my friends are tops – they'd tell you to fuck off!'

'What?' he said, surprised. 'All the girls I know are bottoms. Why are all your friends tops?'

'Because I'm a top!' I explained and my master nodded his understanding. 'Well, actually my friend Aimee would probably have had more fun than I did on Saturday,' I noted. 'At least she's bisexual.'

'Well, then I'd like to see you with her.'

'David!' I protested once again. 'I don't like girls!'

'I know.'

'Why can't you do that with your girlfriend?' I sighed.

'I *do* do that with my girlfriend.'

'How many times?'

'Well, never with a slave,' he answered. 'That was something different. It was good for her to see me top

195

someone. It will make her a better submissive if she understands the other side. We usually get girls who like girls. I guess we've done it, like, ten times maybe.'

'What? If your girlfriend likes doing it and I hate it then why can't you just do it with her?' I asked, baffled.

'That's why I want to do it with you.'

'You want to watch me do things I hate,' I realised.

'Exactly,' he stated, rising onto his relaxed feet to walk over to the open suitcase on the other side of the room.

'Well, you know I'll do whatever you want me to do,' I heard myself say softly.

'Good. Because if you don't you will not be with me,' he continued tonelessly as he folded the T-shirt he'd been wearing, placed it neatly on top of a pile of clothes.

The essence of our relationship came crashing down on me like a heavy whip. David was absolutely serious – our S&M play wasn't a game. He demanded nothing less than complete submission. This wasn't a 'partnership'. There was no 'equality'. David already had a girlfriend – he didn't need another. He didn't want to talk about what I wanted and didn't want to do, but desired only to discuss what was expected of me. And that was that I give him 100% control. It was not up for negotiation. I had graduated. I was now officially 'owned'.

David sidled over to the couch, sat down and motioned for me to come kneel at his feet. 'How long have you been with your girlfriend?' I asked, finally voicing the question that had been taunting me since September.

He thought for a moment. 'Mmm – two and a half years.'

'Oh. How old is she?' I asked, observing the roundness of his strong calves.

'Twenty-nine.'

'And how long have you been with your boyfriend?'

My master paused. 'I broke up with him last month,' he answered slowly.

'Why did you do that?' I asked, startled.

'He's too young. He's only twenty-one – and his girlfriend is really fucked up. She's in competition with me and my girlfriend. She's a bottom who tries to be a top. It's not a good situation.' David paused again before laughing. 'Plus, he likes guys way more than I do!'

I smiled at my master as I rubbed the stubble on his shins. 'So how come you didn't want me to do a threesome with your boyfriend because he's part of your personal life but you make me do a threesome with your girlfriend?' I blurted out.

'Because being with my boyfriend would bring you too much pleasure,' he replied.

'Ahh. Then it's got nothing to do with your personal life.'

David nodded. 'Besides, what I want to do to you, my boyfriend would not have been good for.' As if on cue the buzzer rang. My master reached down and brought my face directly into his own. 'Ah! Candy!' he exclaimed mysteriously before releasing me. 'Eyes down. I don't want you looking until I tell you to look,' he ordered.

Surprised, I obeyed my master, kept my gaze fixed firmly on the floor while he answered the door. I heard footsteps drawing near but didn't dare look up. 'You want a cigarette? Some water?' my master asked.

'No, I'm fine, thanks,' replied the unaccented male voice.

'That's her over there – a very beautiful submissive. You can do whatever you want to do to her. Have a seat. Get a nice foot massage, a good blow job. She'll take very good care of you.'

A body plopped down on the couch in front of me. A hand reached under my chin, tilted my face up to meet the sparkling blue eyes of your average brown-haired boy next door – in Roman times. His Herculean arms and chest were a bit too gladiator for my taste, but who was I to complain? It's the thought that counts – and my master had definitely put some thought into rewarding his slave.

I was overwhelmed with happiness. How many other of my past lovers would have gotten me a stripper for the evening? How many other men who'd entered my life understood my strangest desires? I crawled over to my master and planted a loving kiss on his left foot as he changed porno tapes in the VCR.

'Not me! Him!' he snapped, pointing me back to the couch.

On all fours I shot over to where my naked candy sat playing with his semi-stiff toy. Carefully, I mass-aged one foot then the other before he gently reached down to tilt up my face once more. I felt small as a child as the Herculean hustler opened my mouth, placed his growing cock inside. 'Oh, shit!' the candy cried while my lips moved smoothly along the shaft as naturally as a baby with a bottle. 'Oh, shit! Please, please – whatever you're doing – don't stop!'

I controlled him completely – a Greek god reduced to mere mortal in my mouth – tongue teasing pre-cum from the head, lips circling the base in a lipstick noose as my master's hearty laughter rang deep in my ears. 'I think he likes the way you suck cock! You're a very, very good girl.' Sensing David beside me I gazed upwards, eyes beaming. He smiled proudly. 'You look so beautiful with that big cock in your mouth – very, very beautiful. So pretty,' he praised soothingly.

I continued my cocksucking duty with a fiery determination, every 'Oh, shit! Oh, shit!' uttered from the hustler bringing me closer to my master's heart. 'Relax! Enjoy!' David finally urged in an effort to keep the candy from spilling his juice. 'You've got all night,' he added, then went into the bedroom, returning with rubbers and lube.

My master's strong hands pulled off my panties, poured slick liquid all over my pussy and ass. As his fingers massaged the lube into both holes I felt a burning sensation. 'David!'

'What?'

'It stings!'

'What's "stings"?' David asked unfamiliar with the English word.

'Hurts, man,' the candy explained.

'What is that stuff?'

'I don't know,' my master shrugged. 'Just lube.'

'It hurts, David!'

'OK, OK. Look,' my master calmed like he was addressing a toddler, then tossed the lube into the trashcan. 'All gone.' He went to the bathroom for a towel, hummed softly while soaking it in cold water in the kitchen sink.

'Thank you, sir,' I whispered after he'd tenderly wiped every bit of harsh lubricant from my skin.

'We'll use a different kind,' my master assured. 'Ahh!' he exclaimed, examining the white towel.

'Every time I'm in town she has her period!' His rich laughter echoed as he disappeared into the bedroom, returned to baste me with a bottle of non-acidic Wet instead. After rinsing his hands David opened the refrigerator then sat down at the kitchen table with a sandwich, eating while I sucked. After swallowing the last bite he joined us at the couch. 'OK. My turn now,' he stated, unceremoniously moving his friend aside.

Taking his place on the couch like a king on his throne, my master dragged me by the hair onto his soft cock. Instantly his dick grew hard, expanding like a balloon back to my throat, outwards to my cheeks. He fucked my mouth zealously, the candy kneeling behind me, caressing my body like a velvet cape.

'You look like a monster next to her!' my master exclaimed laughing, then rewarded my hardworking lips with a kiss. 'Tongue!' he demanded, his fist in my hair. 'Stick out your tongue!' David sucked me in like he'd swallow me whole, suddenly releasing my mane with an order to stand. 'Turn around,' he continued and I heard a condom wrapper rip open. 'Sit down.' Carefully I lowered myself onto David's cock. Roughly he forced himself inside my pussy. I whimpered like a dog. 'Suck him!'

Gripping my buttocks like he was guiding the reins of a horse, David thrust hard and deep. The candy's cock throbbing in my throat, I alternated between crying out in pain and gasping for air. 'If you don't stop complaining I'm going to fuck your ass right away. Do you understand me?' my master threatened quietly.

'Yes, sir,' I answered, taking a giant breath.

My master's massive dick sped up inside my wet hole, racing to be first to the ecstatic finish line. The snaps of my leather mini popped open and I felt my skirt being fucked right from my body as the endorphins rushed to my head, David's lion's roar ringing in my ears. Exhausted, my master pushed me up off his dick and went to the bathroom while the candy promptly took his place on the couch. I opened wide for the hustler's anxious cock, playfully weighed its heaviness on my tongue until he brought my mouth up for a lingering kiss.

'What do you want to do to me?' I teased.

'Everything.'

'Well, what specifically? You like S&M? Tying girls up?' I asked sweetly.

'Yeah. David, tie her up!' he shouted to my master.

David returned to the living room and joined us near the couch. 'Why do you want to tie her up?'

'What?'

'You have to give me a reason. I'm not going to tie her up unless you give me a reason,' he matter-of-factly explained.

'Uh, so I can do anything I want to her?'

'Wrong answer,' I blurted before I could catch myself. Fortunately, my master was in agreement, shaking his head before wandering to the refrigerator for more nourishment.

Instead the candy stood up, forcing his dick of steel to the back of my throat like a battering ram until David stopped him. I watched, shocked, as my master nonchalantly encircled Hercules' shaft in his grip. 'No, keep your hand right here,' he directed. 'Fuck her hard, but not too hard. You suck his balls. Right there. Then suck him off.' Having asserted his alpha male prowess my master then went back to eating.

I licked the sweat from Hercules' hairless balls, rolled both appetisers around in my mouth before going for the thick meat. I closed my eyes, listened for the rhythm of his body and tried to tongue to the tune of his never-ending erection. 'You want to come, too?' I finally asked, taking a break since my jaw was killing me.

'I want to fuck you,' the candy panted.

'Well, I'll have to ask my master.'

'David, she has to ask you something,' the candy called.

David kneeled down beside me. 'What do you want?'

'I don't know if he can fuck me,' I whispered like an embarrassed child.

'What are you saying?'

'I don't know if he can fuck me,' I stated louder this time. 'I want to ask your permission.'

'Yes,' David nodded. 'He can fuck you.' Then he returned to the refrigerator again. I waited patiently on my knees while the hustler unwrapped a rubber. 'Hey!' David snapped. 'What are you doing? Put the condom on for him!'

I crawled as quickly as I could over to where the candy was fiddling with a Trojan, offered my services with an open mouth. 'It's better if the partner rolls it on for you,' David explained as my lips slowly smoothed the latex along the length of the fat shaft. 'Sometimes we lose our hard-ons when we stop to put on a condom.' In nearly an entire year of serving my master I had never known him to lose an erection, but who was I to argue when he so enjoyed playing the wise teacher.

The candy pushed me onto the hardwood floor, his impatient cock entering my heated up pussy in a single thrust. 'What's your name?' I asked as his big blue eyes searched mine.

'Trevor. What's yours?'

'Lauren,' I answered as David, stomach satisfied, joined us.

Trevor filled my wet hole with every wide inch of his dick, sweat glistening from the ripped pectorals of his waxed chest like oil. 'Don't look at him!' my master commanded, towering above but watching only me. 'Over here. Look at me,' he ordered, pointing to his hypnotic eyes.

As I locked into his gaze my master entered my soul, fucking me through a fourth hole, while the candy frantically penetrated my body. 'Don't kiss him,' David suddenly said though I wasn't about to. 'You don't look like you're enjoying that too much. Wrap your legs around him. You'd better look like you're enjoying it more than that because if you don't I'm going to come over there right now and fuck you in the ass. Understand?'

'Yes, sir.'

'You ever been fucked by a stranger before?' David asked menacingly.

Well, yeah, actually – lots of times. 'No, sir.'

Trevor concentrated all his energy between my legs to the point of exhaustion. Needing a break, he pulled out his stiff cock and rolled off of me so I scampered up to the couch like a freed dog.

'Stop right there,' David barked. Bewildered, I questioned him with my eyes. 'Now turn back around.' I circled a little to the left and froze. 'When I say turn around I mean one hundred and eighty degrees. That is a thirty-five degree turn!'

'Sorry, sir.' I whirled all the way so that my back was to both hustlers.

'Now bend over – all the way. Ass in the air.' I followed directions so that my bare butt was on display like a tempting dessert. 'Better. Look at that beautiful ass!' David complimented. 'So what else do you want to do to her?'

'Gee, I don't know, man. This is like a dream come true!' the candy answered ecstatically. 'How long do you have her for?'

And that's when I lost it. A fit of giggles welled up from my belly and I doubled over onto the floor in hysterics. My master caught my laughter in spite of himself but Trevor was not amused.

'Aw. People always laugh at me,' he said glumly.

'No! No! I'm not laughing at you!' I protested, not meaning to have offended him. 'I laugh with David all the time!' Then I did just that.

'You let your slave laugh like that?' Trevor finally asked when my non-stop giggles rose to a crescendo, mixing with my master's to fill the small room as David sidled by me to open a window. On his way back to Trevor he nonchalantly reached down, yanked me harshly by the hair to drag me back up to a proper position on my knees.

'Shut up,' he said slowly and fiercely, his nose nearly touching my own.

Stunned silent, I dropped my eyes to the floor, fists tight in two balls by my side. 'Sorry, sir.'

When my master released me to walk to the other side of the room I didn't dare look up. I could only sense his return before hearing the sound of three quick whacks against skin. The burning sensation on my right buttock left by my master's belt reached my brain just as he grabbed me by the hair, jerked me directly into his face once again.

'You think this is a party? This isn't a party! Get to work! Suck him!'

'Yes, sir.'

I made a mad doggy dash to where Trevor sat calmly on the couch, tried to save his deflating erection with cock to mouth resuscitation. David came up behind me, tied my hands back with his belt. As I secured my lips to the candy's recovered dick, tasting its tightness against my tongue, my master applied more lube to my ass, his fingers slowly probing the expanding hole.

'Bad girls get fucked in the ass,' my master whispered in my ear, delivering a stab of anal punishment to his naughty slut.

My shriek of surprise turned into a moan of pain as David rode my ass with his huge cock, sending my body into a rhythm of quake-like rumbles. Blowing Trevor became an exercise in futility so instead I simply rubbed my lips up and down the taut erection from shiny head to smooth balls and back.

'Oh, yeah! Fuck her ass!' Trevor urged as my master disciplined my sore hole with his jackhammer dick, forcing me to the brink of crying mercy. Suddenly he pulled out of my body, unleashed my wrists from his belt. With a sigh I tried to return to Trevor's starved cock but only felt David's hand on my head as I offered my mouth, yanking me away from the candy and back a few feet from the couch.

As I struggled to balance on my knees David maintained his vice grip in my hair, forcing my head up so he could penetrate my eyes while jerking off in my face. When he finally roared, blessing me from forehead to chin with his cum like holy water, I opened wide, licked my lips like catching rain. Then he released me to Trevor so I obediently took the candy's cock into my freshly semen-drenched mouth.

'Tell her to make those sounds she was making

before – when you were fucking her!' the hustler enthused.

'Those were sounds of pain,' I explained, breathing deeply. 'He was hurting me!' After I'd faked a couple of tortured moans, Trevor moved me back to the floor. He stuck his fingers between my lips and I sucked seductively, enjoying his intent gaze glued to my mouth as he played with his pleading dick. 'Your fingers hurt,' I said truthfully when he began to jab my pussy, searching for the elusive pleasure inside.

I glanced over to where my master sat serenely on the couch smoking a cigarette, observing either the Latin porno still screening on the TV or the real one playing just below it, I couldn't tell.

'Hey!' David suddenly barked. 'It's not about her orgasm – it's about you having an orgasm!'

Like a bad boy caught in the cookie jar Trevor instantly took his fingers from my hole. Desperately he tried to jerk off, his hard-on fading fast, finally settling his soft dick in my mouth once again. I was surprised my jaw hadn't become unhinged by now.

'Look, buddy, we've got to wrap this up,' David sighed impatiently. 'I've got to spend some time alone with her and then I've got to go to sleep.' Conceding defeat, the candy rose to get dressed. I crawled onto the couch exhausted, laid my head in my master's lap. 'Hey, can you crack backs?' David asked the hustler while stroking my wild hair.

'I don't know. I've never done it before.'

'Well, I'll show you. I'll do you and then you can do me.'

'OK.'

David stood and picked up Hercules from the floor, cracked his back once he'd taught him the proper breathing method. Though Trevor tried he couldn't do the same for my master. The sight of two naked bodybuilders touching each other made my body hungry for a human sandwich. 'Why is it that I can crack backs but I can't find anyone who can do it to me?' David wondered aloud, oblivious to both my pussy and ass begging for more.

'Maybe if you lay down and got walked on?' I offered helpfully.

David's blank stare went from me to Trevor and back like I'd lost my mind. 'Lauren, the reason Chinese people do that,' he explained like he was addressing a three-year-old, 'is because they are small.'

'No!' I cried. 'I didn't mean him. I meant that *I* could walk on you!'

'Oh,' David laughed. 'Yeah, maybe. Well, thanks for coming over,' my master continued to the candy who'd finished dressing.

'Yeah, thanks,' I added.

'No. Thank you,' Trevor gushed to both of us. 'Can I come back when I'm fresh?' he asked my master on his way out.

David shook his head with a heavy sigh. 'Look, you're not to tell anyone about this. OK?'

'No, of course not,' the hustler agreed before David shut the door on him. He turned around to lock into my eyes, a huge grin gracing his handsome face. The smug smile never left his lips as he walked jauntily to the refrigerator and poured a glass of water.

'What?' I finally asked, beaming as well.

'Nothing,' David shrugged.

'You are the best master in the world,' I declared, emphasising every word.

'And why is that?'

'Because you're perfect.'

'I try to be.'

David brought his water, a protein bar and an orange over to where I sat still buzzing on the comfy couch and positioned his solid body on the hardwood floor between my legs. 'Massage?' I guessed.

David nodded as he tore into his protein bar. I laid my hands on his strong shoulders, lost my fingers in every sculpted muscle. 'Way,' my master praised.

'You know, I didn't even get to touch you on Saturday,' I whispered in his ear, my palms stroking the feathers of his wings.

'I know,' he replied before switching to the couch so I could caress his lower half.

Straddling the backs of my master's powerful thighs, I thrust my hips up and down in an effort to massage the hard globes of his buttocks. 'I'm topping you,' I continued in a whisper. 'I'm fucking your ass.'

'Way,' David murmured before I melted into his flesh, my eyelids too heavy to keep open.

'David, I'm falling asleep. And it's raining outside so I don't want to have to try for a car service. Can I crash over here?' I slurred.

'I was just about to ask you what you want to do.'

'That's OK? I don't work on Fridays so I can get up whenever you do,' I added.

'That's fine,' he yawned.

'OK, I'm going to sleep then.' And with that I rolled off my master, planted a tender kiss on his forehead, removed my leather corset and stumbled into the bedroom. Curled up under the covers, I started to doze just as I felt my master slip between the sheets. 'No *Se7en*?' I mumbled dreamily.

'It's right here.'

David hit 'play' on his portable DVD and Brad Pitt thanked Morgan Freeman in French. I fell in and out of sleep with the ringing of the phone as horny clients had to make do with my master's voice on a machine.

At eleven in the morning I awoke to a buzzing sound. David got up and began talking through the intercom in French. Then he crawled back into bed.

'What was that?'

'The door.'

'Yeah, I know that. Do you have a client? Why were you speaking in French?' I pried.

'No, no client. That was Max, my ex.'

'He's coming up?' I wondered worriedly.

'No, no,' David assured.

'You still talk to him?'

'Sure,' he said with a shrug.

We went back to sleep for another hour until I woke once again with a start. 'Oh, wow! I just had a nightmare.'

'What was it about?' David asked, enclosing me in his safe arms.

'I dreamt you made me fuck Roxanne.'

'Well, then that is a very good dream,' he corrected. 'We should do it.'

'No, it's not a good dream,' I stated firmly. 'Roxanne's the type of girl who will tell a guy to go down on her and then kick him out without reciprocating. You would not like her.'

'Hmmm. Then I think I would like to fuck her in the ass, jerk off on her face and kick her out.'

'That's why you'll never be with Roxanne.' We both climbed drowsily out of bed and I dressed as David fixed a bowl of oatmeal in the kitchen then flopped onto the couch in front of the TV. 'What are you watching?'

'*Rush Hour*,' he replied as I pottered about the room, picking up the pieces of my wardrobe from the night before. 'So how come all your friends don't fuck?'

'No, they do fuck. They just don't fuck your type,' I clarified. 'They don't like the guys at the Gaiety. They don't like muscles. They're more into the Leonardo DiCaprio/Ricky Martin thing.'

'That's awful!' David exclaimed, choking on his oatmeal.

'I know. I'm totally the opposite. I like manly macho men.'

'Well, all the Gaiety dancers are macho but it's not real – it's a fake macho.'

'Yeah, I hate that. Insecurity is the biggest turn off.' After slipping back into my leather corset and mini I sat on the couch beside my master and watched Chris Tucker run after an Asian baddie. 'You know, I shot my first porno Saturday night.'

'You mean filming us?'

'Yeah.'

'And how was it?'

'Awful. I hated it,' I pouted.

'Good.'

'I mean, it's frustrating being forced to watch other people do what you want to be doing but can't. I want to be the centre of attention all the time! I want it to always be all about me!' I cried.

'Well, it can't be all about you all the time,' David said matter-of-factly.

'But I want it to be.'

'Well, it can't.' My master continued to eat while the baddies got away.

I sighed resignedly. 'I hate it but you make me happy.'

'Good.'

'I'll do whatever you want me to do.'

'That is your job.'

'So how come you never bring a whip with you if you want to whip me?' I asked, suddenly curious.

David shot me a look like I was loony. 'I am not going to bring a whip across the border!'

'Why not? It's not illegal.'

'I know – but if I bring a whip then they'll start looking for other violent things. I don't even bring pot across the border.'

'Well, I think I would like you to whip me,' I continued. 'I think I would like you to leave marks on my ass,' I purred as my master smiled, satisfied. 'That dancer you got me last night – he's American, right?'

'He's from Montreal.'

'Really? I thought he was American. He doesn't have a French accent.'

'He's just Canadian – not French-Canadian,' David explained.

I phoned for a car as David finished breakfast. 'Ten minutes? Fine. Call me when they get here. Thanks.' The minute I hung up, my master ordered me down to the floor in front of his growing dick. He brought both my breasts over the top of the corset, bit harshly into my tender nipples. I clenched my teeth as he rubbed my clit through my panties, tried to concentrate on the pleasure from his fingers and ignore the pain from his mouth. 'I want you to fuck me!' I begged in ecstasy.

Forcefully David pushed me away, grabbed his cock and shoved it into my mouth. He conquered the wet hole until he was on the edge of coming. 'That's enough!'

The phone rang like Cinderella's clock chiming midnight so I returned my breasts to their tight binding, put on my long leather coat. My master pointed to his lips. I knelt to kiss him then headed for the door.

'I'll call you,' he added.

I nodded. 'Remember – you still have to rape me,' I reminded, attempting cheer.

Inside the Metroline car I drifted dreamily back to Brooklyn, awakening blocks from my apartment to take fifteen dollars from my purse. Outside my building I paid the driver and stepped into the sunshine, smiling sweetly at my hot Czech neighbour as I bounded up the stairs, hair untamed and bitch stockings showing. I didn't care what anyone thought of me. I was a sex toy – a kinky slave to be used. And I was a damn good one.